The House on Dead Man's Curve

Jason Roach

The House on Dead Man's Curve

This book is loosely based off personal paranormal experiences by the author. The characters and main events portrayed in this book are fictitious. Any similarity to real persons, living or dead, is coincidental and not intended by the author.

Hardcover ISBN-13: 979-8-9868862-2-0
Paperback ISBN-13: 979-8-9868862-1-3
e-book ISBN-13: 979-8-9868862-0-6

Edited by: Lynn Picknett
Cover design by: Hannah Barnhardt
Formatting by: Polgarus Studio
Printed in the United States of America

To Sean - without your love and support,
this book would have never happened.

ACKNOWLEDGMENTS

I would like to start by giving a huge thanks to my editor, Lynn Picknett. Thank you for all your support, guidance and friendship. To my cover artist, Hannah Barnhardt, thank you for all your hard work and ability to create some of the most amazing artwork. To Alex Matsuo, thank you for being an inspiration, paranormal leader, and friend. To Patrick Dugan, Darin Kennedy and Matthew Saunders, thank you for taking the time to assist a rookie. And lastly, but definitely not least, thank you for purchasing and reading this book.

Prologue

The glow of blue, red, and white flashing lights from the emergency vehicles and police cars broke up the darkness that cloaked the area. Sirens killed the natural silence that would normally encompass the country road, alerting those in the area that an accident of some sort had occurred. Orange and white roadblock signs were set up in both the north and south bound lanes to keep any traffic from coming through, and plastic yellow tape that read "POLICE LINE DO NOT CROSS" was hung up around the perimeter. The marked-off area was relatively wide considering the circumference of the sharp curve where the incident had occurred and the distance that the two-story house sat back from the road. In the ditch rested a car that was so beat up from being t-boned and overturned several times that it was hardly recognizable. The side-by-side black skid marks filled the air with the stench of burning rubber being dragged across the asphalt, stopping at the wreckage of the freight truck that had plowed into the car. There was only one survivor.

Walking out of the darkness, a tall older gentleman with broad shoulders snuck behind one of the fire trucks and grabbed a fireman's jacket and hat lying on the back of the truck, quickly putting them on. He took a deep breath and casually stumbled out from behind the truck as if he was supposed to be there. Slowly making his way over to the police chief, who was directing the search for clues in different areas of the location, he thought to himself that somehow, he needed to distract the searchers to prevent them from finding out certain things, at least until he could make sure all loose ends were cleaned up.

"Howdy, sir," he said to the police chief. "I'mma sorry for, uh, bein' late. Where'd ya, uh…?"

"Not a problem. I appreciate you coming in on such

short notice. It's a mess out here," the police chief replied, looking over the perimeter where multiple emergency vehicles were lined around the bend. "Why don't you take point over there and start searching along the far tree line over on the right side of the house? Look for anything that might tell us what the hell happened out here."

"Sure, uh, yeah, I'mma gon' 'ver there," the imposter fireman replied.

This was his chance. He was glad the police chief had sent him directly into the area where he wanted to be and knew exactly what he was looking for. As he approached, he slowly combed through the thickets and trees that lined the far-right side of the property.

It wasn't long before he found traces of what he was looking for. The first clue was a cell phone that appeared to have been tossed to the ground during some kind of struggle. He picked it up, looked around to see if anyone was watching, then turned it off and quickly placed it in one of the deep pockets of his overalls. There now. That was one thing he needed to get rid of. All he had to do now was locate where the cell phone had come from. About fifteen yards away, he found the answer - lying under a tree.

"Well, now, Ma'am. You thunk I was just gon' let ya get uh way?" the broad-shouldered man said, moving closer to the near lifeless body lying sprawled on the ground. He could see there were still signs of life as the woman's chest moved up and down with slow shallow breaths. There was a puddle of blood beneath her which had poured from the gunshot wound that had clearly entered her back and exited through her stomach. He was careful not to step in or get it on his clothes as he kneeled beside her. The woman started to grunt while trying to push her body away with her legs, but before she could make enough noise to draw attention to him, the man pulled out an old handkerchief from his back pocket. He placed it over her face, sealing it tightly with his hand, and holding it hard until the once breathing body lay there completely lifeless. Now his secret was safe. He stuffed the handkerchief back down into his pocket, so deep that it wouldn't fall out.

He looked up to see another set of emergency workers carrying out two other bodies down the front steps of the house, one wrapped in a white sheet and the other a comforter. He wasn't worried: They'd been there for over a week, and neither could provide the police with clues that might lead back to him. He messed up the earth with his feet where the victim had tried to move her legs and feet to obliterate any signs of a struggle. After hastily rechecking there were no signs of life, he called out to the other rescue workers.

"Hey! Ova here! Got 'nother one!"

Another group of first responders came running over from a nearby ambulance with their medical bags and he slowly stepped back to let them in. As they worked on the lifeless body, checking for a pulse and taking pictures of the area, he noticed that the focus was no longer on him, and he took this chance to slip back into the darkness. Far away from what would soon be known as the crime scene of the century and would continue to add to the lore of Dead Man's Curve.

Night One

Monday October 25th, 2021

"Later, team! Have a great week!" Tyler Drewitt said over his shoulder, walking out of his gray cubicle to leave the office. He was excited to be taking a week's vacation away from the draining world of accounts payable and tedious water-cooler gossip - and heading on a paranormal investigation with research team leader Emily Adair. Emily had founded the Winston Salem Paranormal Research Group many years before, but Tyler had just recently joined. He had been interested in the paranormal ever since he was a child watching *The X Files,* not to mention some of the more personal encounters he had experienced over his forty years.

When he was a young boy, he remembered attending the funeral of his maternal grandmother. Because he was so young, his parents did not allow him to attend the graveside service following the hellfire and brimstone beatdown given by the officiant. His paternal aunt whisked him away before the second service could begin, but not before he took one last look at the rest of the family gathering around the gravesite. Waving back at him from behind the enormous oak tree, stood his grandmother - the woman his parents told him was no longer with the living. Just as quickly as she had peered around the tree, she disappeared. When he told others what he'd seen, they laughed, telling him it was a figment of his childhood imagination. But he knew what he'd seen - his grandmother, looking young and well, waving to him. His grandmother, who his family had just buried.

Tyler didn't have another paranormal experience until he was in his early twenties. He was helping a friend clean a new house she had just rented. They were both in separate rooms across the hall from one another. The front door was left open in anticipation of the landlord stopping by. Deep in their work, Tyler - out of the corner of his eye - caught a dark shadow moving down the hall. Not fully clear on what he'd seen, he went into the hallway to investigate. He and his friend looked at each other from their perspective doorways. She'd seen it too. They searched the house high and low, thinking the landlord had arrived, but to no avail. Their search turned up nothing and the landlord never showed up that day.

Other experiences included - but were not limited to - seeing a woman in eighteenth century clothing walking up the hill to his house while he was mowing the lawn lower down. Other times, weirdly, what appeared to be old radio shows could be heard from various parts of his home. When he investigated it, the shows seemed to travel from room to room, but Tyler knew he didn't own a radio. Coming full circle, the sounds stopped when he reached the starting point of his search. He experienced this frequently when coming home from a night out - so the house was completely dark.

There are those who refuse to believe in the afterlife or paranormal, but because of his vivid and unexplained personal experiences, Tyler wasn't one of them. The mere definition of paranormal is an event beyond the scope of current scientific explanation. If that didn't fit his experiences, he didn't know what else could. Then there was the vexed subject of spirits, ghosts or whatever term one might use. Outside of Halloween pranks, and juvenile 'woo-woo' jokes, it was a deeply serious issue - as Tyler had cause to know.

He sometimes felt that spirits can cross over - from wherever they might be - into our realm to convey a message. Maybe to tell us what had actually occurred on a certain date or to give us a warning about something that could endanger our lives. Some people believe spirits are stuck here after death as a penance for a lifestyle of wrongdoing, and others believe in what is known as residual energy, where an event in history replays itself over and over - though the two are not mutually exclusive.

Gettysburg would be considered an example of residual energy, where sounds and even sights of the battle are said to be experienced by visitors. Tyler wasn't sure about the penance, but he did have a strong belief in residual energy. He wondered if this would be predominant during the investigation.

Trying to push his claustrophobia from his mind - he hated tight spaces -, Tyler pulled out his phone as he entered the small elevator to head the three floors down to the lobby. He sent Emily a quick text to let her know that he would be on the road shortly after getting home and packing up his gear.

The forty-five-minute drive home to Winston Salem was packed with traffic, and while navigating through the cars and transfer trucks, he made a checklist of everything he needed to load into the car before heading out. Top priorities were the digital voice recorder, camcorder, Flir thermal imagery camera, and the back-up batteries he had left scattered all over his apartment to charge were all back in his equipment case.

Hoooooonnnnkkkk! The sound of the car horn

pulled Tyler out of his daydreaming checklist to find he had veered into the lane of oncoming traffic and had nearly had a head on collision. “Sorry! Sorry!” he said as he pulled his Blue 2019 Honda Civic back into his lane. “Best not to become a ghost before you get to investigate them”, he said, chuckling at the irony. He popped in the latest Tori Amos album to keep him more alert as he traveled down the road. He was nearly home and preferred to stay alive long enough to make it there.

Arriving home, he jumped into the shower, got changed and began to gather the things off his checklist and load them into the car. He grabbed his Macbook and placed it on the counter where he could quickly review the information on the location the team would be investigating the following week. As the computer loaded, he ran more items out to the car, fixed himself a water to go, and then sat down in the high-top chair at the counter. He pulled up the group's communication page and began to review the information he’d already read multiple times but had to ensure he had it all down. He wanted to make a good impression with the team as this was his first full-on extended investigation.

The site they'd be investigating was an old farmhouse turned Airbnb, on a manor-like estate in the outskirts of Statesville. Only about forty minutes away from Tyler's home in Winston Salem, it was known as "the city of progress" - but in his opinion the city had made very little of it over the years. Aside from areas dedicated to shopping and a small historic downtown quarter, it was mostly surrounded by old farmlands. The area, though, would be quite nice this time of year. Mid-October brought the changing of the leaves into a riot of fall colors, all around the highways and streets. It also brought colder temperatures… "God! I hope this place is heated," he thought fervently. The temperatures for the week were set to be some of the coldest for this early into the season, though North Carolina has long tended to mostly skip fall and jump straight into winter.

The house was located on a long road where one way led straight into town and the other led farther and farther out into the country, with nothing but trees, fields, cattle, farmhouses - and where, at night, the darkness of the night sky quickly devoured the area, leaving no trace of light for miles. The house sat in the exact center of a sharp curve in the road that had come to be known as "Dead Man's Curve." Certainly sounded ominous.

Over the years all the houses in the vicinity had experienced some kind of paranormal activity, including, it was said, an old fort dating from the French and Indian War way back in the mid-eighteenth century. Hopefully, this could be looked into during the day, when places were open for research. He loved local history and hoped time would permit him to pay a visit to the old fort.

Tyler, deeply absorbed in reading the history of the area, realized he had lost track of time and jumped up from the chair, grabbed his all-important laptop, and did a quick check to make sure everything was already in the car. He typed the address into his iPhone, plugged it into the car, and backed out of the driveway. He stopped at the end to quickly text Emily that he was running behind but was on his way. He set the music to yet another Tori Amos album and drove off. He was on his way to the investigation of his life and couldn't wait to see what mysteries and unexplained activities would occur.

Tyler was your average forty-year-old male. He stood roughly five foot nine inches tall, had short dark hair, which was always a bit of a mess and was receding slightly, and an increasingly slackening dad bod. When not working, he was a bit of a loner, and when around other people, the interactions became kinda awkward at times as he would make random references to stuff they'd never heard of. His obsession with - and fanboy's obscure references to - Harry Potter were the usual culprits. He mostly stayed home listening to music and researching odd topics on the internet when he wasn't lost in the YouTube or Tik Tok black holes. When he did watch TV, he was glued to any paranormal show he could find. It was how he learned what to do during investigations so that he didn't seem entirely oblivious. It was also how he learned how not to act so he didn't look even more insensible.

This one was going to be different than any he experienced so far. Sure, he had done the occasional public investigation, where large historical locations would open up for groups of twenty or so more people to conduct a chaperoned investigation. There was even the time when he got to spend the night on the Battleship *North Carolina* off the coast of Wilmington - where he saw a dark shadow figure rush down one of the corridors out of the corner of his eye - but the investigation he was heading towards now was the epic of all epics, at least in his mind. He was going to be spending a whole seven days in a so-called haunted house. Not only that, but it also happened to be the week of Halloween. They had the whole property to themselves from Monday night till the following Monday morning. Tyler was probably a little over enthusiastic about this, but he didn't care. His teammates would just have to deal with it. He was going to make the most he could out of his week in the house.

Tyler's only concern for the week was Emily. While he adored her, there was a past of tension between the two of them. They had known each other for a while but had never been confined together for a long period of time. Her strong A Type personality tended to intimidate him at times. He knew she didn't mean any harm; it was just her nature. She stood no taller than five foot four with shoulder length blonde hair, which she normally kept pulled up in a ponytail on the top of her head - she was a bit of a tomboy, having been raised by her father after her mother had left them. She was something of an enigma, not being given to effusive emotions or small talk, but her knowledge of the paranormal earned Tyler's utmost respect for her. Her knowledge of conducting paranormal investigations was out of this world, and far better than you would see on TV.

Emily was methodological about investigating and - even better, in his eyes - her passion came from paranormal experiences she too had as a child. Her experiences started off in the non-denominational church she was forced to attend when visiting her mother. There were occasions as a teenager that Emily was accused by the church of being possessed by the devil because she didn't bend to their beliefs. It all came to a head during youth group, when multiple fellow teens, along with the leader, held her down against her will and proceeded to attempt to cast the devil out of her. While they commanded devils to come out of her and spoke in gibberish "tongues", Emily kicked and screamed, desperate to get away, but she couldn't budge the grip they had on her hands and feet. Fighting the tears pouring down her face, she opened her eyes - but immediately wished she hadn't... Instead of teen faces contorted with hysterical hate, there were dark shadowy faces, and solid dark entities looming menacingly over the group. It was at this moment she realized she wasn't the one with the devils: the true "possessed" ones were those projecting hate onto her for not conforming to what they believed she should be. Emily decided the only way out of this nightmare was to briefly give into their desires. She stopped fighting them and remained still, tears still running down her cheeks, until the group of teenagers and group leaders decided to see her submissiveness as a victory and praised Jesus for her deliverance. Understandably, she never stepped foot in church again. However, making this decision also put a strain on the relationship with her mother, who to this day continues to view her daughter through the church's eyes. An evil one.

Engrossed with the memory of the dark spirits around those who held her down some years before, she decided to start the paranormal research group to obtain evidence that would prove to others - things happen which we can't always explain in normal, everyday terms. Things that control how others act. Therefore, to be as persuasive and objective as possible, everything had to be well documented. Any noise that could be construed as paranormal but turned out not to be, had to be tagged in the audio so that whoever was reviewing would know it wasn't otherworldly. Surveillance cameras had to be placed in the perfect spot in order to capture as much of the location as possible. The most important aspect was that respect had to be shown to both the living and the dead. As he drove, Tyler fervently hoped that the respect also extended to members of her team.

Tyler veered off the highway exit that would lead him to the main road where the house was supposed to be located. GPS said there were only two miles to go. The sun was nearly gone, and a velvety darkness was taking over the sky. The outline of the trees could barely be seen, and the only light was coming from an old gas station that had seen better days, maybe in the 1950's. He made the right hand turn as the GPS directed, switching on his high beams so that hopefully he could identify the house from the pictures in the team's information pack. He drove slowly as this was uncharted territory and wanted to make sure that he didn't miss the driveway.

According to the GPS the destination should be just up ahead, but he couldn't see anything except open pastures and trees. There was a small, rundown old graveyard next to a one-room chapel. "Man, rundown must be the thing around here," he thought after passing a historical land marker sign - which he could barely read until he almost had his nose on it - apparently for an old schoolhouse, but even then, it passed by too fast. "Guess I'll have to check that out during the daytime," he thought. He continued to drive slower when suddenly, the road began to bend. He knew the house was supposed to be located in the center of Dead Man's Curve. All he could see was a line of trees, but as he nearly got on top of them, he slammed on his brakes. "Jesus!" Tyler yelled. Smack dab in the middle of this curve was a dark driveway lined with the thick red and orange glow of crape myrtles on both sides. No one could have seen this ahead of time - perhaps why it was such an accident black spot. Frustrated at almost missing the turn, shakily he slowly pulled in.

The picture had made it seem that the house sat almost on the road, but that wasn't the case. The driveway appeared to go back for at least a half a mile. Driving in he spotted Emily's car and pulled up beside it. And there she was, still sitting in it in the dark. He wondered where the rest of the team was. Maybe he wasn't as late as he'd feared. Or maybe everyone else was running behind too. He thought about placing some kind of a marker at the entrance to the driveway so that the others didn't have the same problem spotting it from the road. He and Emily both started to get out of the car at the same time.

"Hey! Sorry I'm running behind. Have you been here long?" he said.

"Nah. I just got here myself. Man, what a turn up there! I thought I was going to cause an accident. Had to slam the brakes on hard to make that turn," Emily responded, starting to unload the equipment and her suitcase of clothes.

"Right! That was a mess." Tyler looked around, feeling a distinct chill - and not just from the evening air. "It's creepy out here. All I hear are crickets and cows. Where are the others?"

"Well… apparently Dawn and Kit can't make it. I'm not really sure what's going on there, but it looks like it's just the two of us. Can you give me a hand with the surveillance equipment?"

Tyler felt a rumble of nervousness travel through his body at the thought of it just being the two of them for the week. He'd hoped this worst-case scenario would not occur. He decided he would make the best of it. At least the house was big enough for them to go their separate ways should the need arise.

"Oh yeah, for sure! Here let me...Whoa!" Tyler spun around, suddenly aware of the house looming in the evening gloom. Now he felt rising excitement, tempered with more than a little apprehension - after all, there were just the two of them now.

`The house stood off to the right of the driveway's end, with three broken-up brick steps leading up to the cracked and weed-eaten path to the front porch. Now he focused on it properly, the house was dark and gray, or at least that's how it appeared in the near-total blackness. Even though it stood two stories high, there was no way it could be seen from the road in this dark. And the longer he stood there, the more sinister it got. Tyler thought that maybe once the lights were on it would be a little better - but right now there was an uneasy feeling down in his gut. He found himself looking over his shoulder in case something was creeping up on him.

Emily reached the front door first after climbing yet another set of concrete steps onto the porch, which was wide and rickety and stretched the entire length of the front of the house. It creaked ominously as she stepped on it, setting her suitcase down. The boards were beginning to rot, and the paint had obviously been flaking off for some time now.

"The owner was supposed to leave the key somewhere around here," Emily said, as she turned on her phone's flashlight and looked around for any hidden nooks where a key might be hidden. After a few minutes, she finally found a little black box clipped to the top of an old rocking chair.

"That's a random place to put a key. Not hidden very well, is it?" Tyler said, adding, "Unless you count the darkness. Then everything is hidden."

"They said it would be easy to find when I messaged them on the Airbnb app. Kinda odd that they didn't want to meet us here beforehand, but I guess that's how Airbnb's work these days."

"Don't get me wrong, I'm totally grateful we get to be here, but should this place even be an Airbnb? It's not like it's the safest place to be staying, and we haven't even made it inside yet." Tyler replied, hauling another load of equipment onto the porch. "Aren't there guidelines and codes…and stuff… they would need to follow?

“You would think so, but then again it doesn’t really look like their PR pictures either”

Emily removed the key from the little black box and walked over to the door. However, as she went to insert it into the deadbolt, the door creakingly opened ever so slightly. “Well, that’s interesting,” she murmured, shining her flashlight into the dark doorway, expecting to find someone on the other side to greet them.

“Say what?” Tyler asked, arriving back after his last trip from the car.

“The door just opened on its own. It wasn’t even locked.”

“You know, if this wasn’t supposed to be a haunted house, I'd be asking for a refund real quick,” Tyler declared, unsure of what to expect on the other side, but oblivious to the fact most people would ask for a refund because it *was* a haunted house.

Emily smiled to herself in the gloom. That was actually quite sweet. But she said nothing, bustling around and adding briskly: “Right! Let me see if I can find a light switch or something so that we can see what we're doing."

Emily felt around the door frame, eventually locating the old-style raised switch. With the light on, she helped Tyler carry in the rest of the equipment and suitcases from the porch, lining them up on the polished wood floor just inside the door. They, then, decided to do a walkthrough to check out the best places to set up the surveillance cameras.

Upon entering the house there were two rooms on either side of the hallway. The first on the right was a medium-sized living area with an old Victorian sofa with wood trimmings and decorative claw foot legs. There was a fireplace with a thin black metal screen over the fireplace plus wrought iron accessories. Double windows with sheer curtains hanging down to the floor, lined the wall to their right, looking out onto the porch. A closet door was all there was on the far-left wall.

"This definitely looks more appealing than the outside," Tyler said, pointing out that the top of the fireplace would be a great place for a camera. Emily agreed, then they headed to the room across the hall, which was dominated by a king size bed with two nightstands on each side, under windows that in daylight would give an open view to the driveway where the cars were parked. To their left large double windows with sheer curtains hanging to the floor again faced out onto the porch. To their right was a caddy-cornered early 20th century cherry-stained armoire next to a closet door. They both agreed that a view of the room from the top of the armoire would be the perfect angle for surveillance.

The two of them walked into the hallway, past the staircase on the right that led to the second floor. There was a small, hinged cupboard door that was maybe just tall enough for an eight- or nine-year-old to fit in. "Look! It even comes with its own Harry Potter cupboard," Tyler remarked. Emily just smiled vaguely, saying swiftly, "So some of the stories are that people hear the stairs creak on their own in the middle of the night."

"That's interesting," Tyler replied, realizing his Harry Potter comment had either gone over Emily's head or she was just ignoring it all together. She tended to be more focused on business during investigations than swapping flippancies.

Emily made off into the next room on the left which turned out to be a somewhat formal dining room. As they walked in, she asked Tyler, "So I know you've done a couple of small investigations with us now. How are you feeling about that? What's some of your favorite highlights? What really fuels your fire when it comes to the paranormal?"

Tyler thought long and hard to answer her, while noticing the cherry-stained dining room table - where he imagined spending a large amount of time reviewing evidence during the week. "I think I'm feeling pretty good about joining. I've learned a lot while doing the smaller investigations. I think one of my favorite parts is learning to navigate the tech side of it. I've always been a techie in some ways. The fuel to the fire though is really trying to get answers to questions that I've had ever since my own experiences."

"Ok. Great!" Emily said. "We've enjoyed having you along. This will be a great chance for you to test your tech expertise since it's just the two of us. But when you say experiences, what level of paranormal are we talking about?"

They had talked about this prior to Tyler joining the team, but not in very much detail. He had always kept his experiences more internal than external. However, if there was ever a time to explain, this would be perfect as there was no one else around to judge him. "Well, I saw a full-body apparition once. That was the main one. It walked into my room and stood there looking at me. I didn't really look up from the book I was reading, because I thought it was my ex-partner coming in. When I went to see what he wanted, I noticed he was wearing completely different clothing than whomever had come into my room. I'd like to think that it was my grandfather who had come back to check on me - because my living situation was not ideal at the time - but I'm just not sure. Aside from that, I've experienced the occasional shadow moving out of the corner of my eye, but that presence in my room left me completely puzzled."

Fascinated, Emily leaned on the back of a dining chair. "Those are really great experiences. Most people who are interested in the paranormal would love to report something like that. My experiences have been much darker, but the most exciting ones occurred while working with the Rhine Research Center in Durham. I'll have to tell you about them sometime. But it was while doing research with the Rhine on demonic possession that I started documenting all my experiences, which led to me starting the team." Tyler saw her look of discomfort when she mentioned a darker experience. He was intrigued - what did she mean by "darker"? But best not to pry: no doubt she'd tell him when she was ready. If she ever felt comfortable with him, that is. Taking the chance to quickly change the subject, as he himself was not completely comfortable talking about his own experiences, he said, "That cherry china cabinet in the corner is gorgeous. Cherry wood is my favorite stain".

The room had a very hospitable feel with the buffet and display cases being filled with silver plated paraphernalia. They both looked around appreciatively, then Emily mentioned this room would be better covered by a mini digital video (DV) camcorder on a tripod in the far corner by the closet door. The battery would need to be monitored as they only lasted three hours each. Tyler was not looking forward to changing batteries so often and hoped that he could convince her otherwise.

"You know, I'm not trying to overstep any boundaries here, but I think it may be better to just place a surveillance camera on top of the china cabinet looking down from the far right-hand corner of the room." Tyler said timidly, "I just don't think it's logistically feasible to change a DV battery every three hours."

"You are correct, and you have passed part one of tonight's tech exam," Emily smirked, wheeling smartly around to leave the dining room.

Across the hall was the kitchen. Counters lined the back wall with all kitchen amenities - sink, stove, coffee pot and microwave. A large island was the center focal point with four bar stools, two on each side. An old retro-looking fridge was right next to the double doored pantry. They both agreed this would be where they would set up their command center, with the surveillance monitors and equipment scattered across the kitchen. Creature comforts were provided for - cases of water stored in the fridge, and of course one could not forget the snacks, absolute essentials for any self-respecting investigator.

After moving all the equipment from the hall to the kitchen, they headed up the stairs. Each hardwood step creaked under their weight. Surrounding the top was a fence-like railing that effectively created an upstairs hallway. The bathroom was immediately to the right when you reached the top. It too was filled with all the amenities including: his and her sinks, shower, and a fully stocked open linen closet. It's unlikely they'd need surveillance here, so the two of them exited the room after giving it a quick glance.

"What are some of the other stories about weird stuff happening in this house?" Tyler asked, as they turned toward the bedroom across the hall.

"Well, aside from the creaking stairs, people have seen the apparition of an old lady looking out of various front windows. There have also been reports of apparitions walking down the road just before the curve out front. It's said they are there to warn people of the dangers of the bend."

"I wonder what the old lady's story is?'' Tyler queried. Emily hesitated slightly, then responded, "The rumor is that she inherited the house from its original owners. People aren't sure whether she was a relative, a worker, or a friend of the family at the time. This is something I would like to find out."

"I'm sure we could uncover something if we dig hard enough. County records would be a great place to start, but I don't think they open till like nine in the morning," Tyler said.

"We might also find stuff around the house that might help us out." Emily said, turning on the light in the small bedroom across the hall. The furniture was minimal and basic. Since there was nothing particularly high up, they would need to set up a surveillance camera on a tripod to get a good view of the entire room.

Moving up the hall towards the front of the house, they entered the next room on the right. Upon turning on the light, their jaws dropped at the well-stocked home library. The glass doored cherry-stained bookcases engulfed every available wall space, except for the double windows that faced out over the front yard. Double windows on the wall opposite this entryway also looked out over the driveway and into an open field with a dense line of trees towards the back. In the center of the room was a reading area with two wood framed Victorian wingback chairs flanking a table and lamp. It made for a nice cozy spot to sit and read one of the many books that filled the bookcases - which might prove to be very useful.

"Well, here's your chance to find out about the house. I bet there's all kinds of juicy information in these old books," Tyler said, longingly running his fingers across a glass case. "Some of these books go back to the mid-eighteen hundreds. When did the information pack say this house was built?" Looking across from browsing through the bookcases on the opposite side of the room, Emily said "I want to say it was built just prior to the Civil War, but I'm not one hundred percent sure. This structure doesn't appear to be that old, though."

"I definitely plan on spending some time in this room tomorrow. I want to see what we can dig up in here," Tyler said, before pointing out that they could position cameras on bookcases to cover the whole room for activity. They both walked out of what they'd dubbed "The Library" and headed towards the room across the hall that appeared to be a master bedroom.

This medium-sized room was roughly the same dimensions as the living room directly underneath it. Another brick fireplace mirrored the same setup as just a few feet below. The room was dominated by the king size bed placed against the left wall with matching light-grained wood nightstands on either side. Another closet door was on the far-right side of the wall next to the nightstand. They yet again picked the fireplace as the best place to set up the cameras to cover the whole room.

After the tour they headed back downstairs and began to get all the surveillance kits in place. Tyler was running the wires and positioning the cameras, while Emily was setting up the monitors and DVR in the kitchen. They worked mostly in silence, with the occasional walkie interruption to double check the angles and views were as perfect as they could get. While Tyler was setting up the last room, the library, he balanced precariously on a fold-out chair to reach the top of the bookcase, but when he turned to untangle one of the camera wires, he thought he saw Emily go into the master bedroom and close the door. He yelled out to see if she was ok but there was no response. Concerned, he picked up his walkie and tried to reach her that way. "Emily, girl, you ok?" he asked.

"Yeah, I'm fine. I'm just down here trying to figure out all these cords. You probably just heard me trip over one," Emily replied through the walkie.

"Umm, actually, well…Yeah, that's probably what it was. Sorry. Holler if you need me. I'm gonna finish getting these cameras set up and head back down there." Tyler had just broken one of the team's major rules - not to instantly report a weird experience - though he did at least reopen the door to peek into the room, checking if anyone was in there. Seeing no one, he went back to setting up his cameras in the library.

When he returned to the kitchen, he found Emily struggling to plug the monitor into the DVR. He looked at her pointedly, saying "Umm… Emily… If you're still trying to figure out how to plug in the monitor, how did you know when to tell me if the cameras were all lined up?"

"You haven't asked me about lining up the cameras yet, have you?" Emily replied, as Tyler took over and inserted each end of the power cords into the monitor and DVR. When the screen came on, the cameras were all shown on the screens and were perfectly aligned.

"Well, someone responded to me while I was doing it. Apparently, the ghosts are ready for the show," Tyler said, it finally dawning on him to be completely puzzled about the encounter he'd just had upstairs.

"Just kidding! You have now passed test number two for the exam," Emily said, laughing.

"Well, looky there. You can joke around, after all.

What a revelation! Why aren't you like this with the rest of the team?" Tyler asked.

Emily seemed reluctant to answer, starting to clean up the mess she'd created in the kitchen. "I don't know. I guess I feel like I need to maintain some kind of composure around the team, but even I've been known to indulge in the occasional joke every now and then"

"So now we're all set up, where are we going to sleep? I'm about ready to crash for the night." Tyler yawned, walking out to the lobby to grab his bag.

"I think I'd like to try out the master bedroom upstairs," Emily said, as she picked up her suitcase. "Why don't you take the bedroom right here?"

"Yeah, ok cool. I can do that, and, since we're here for the week, we can change rooms if we decide to," Tyler replied, dragging his stuff into the bedroom. "Want any help with carrying your suitcase up the stairs?"

"Nah, I think I'm good. Cameras are running so we should be good to download and review in the morning. I'll see you then. Get some rest. We're gonna need it."

Emily lugged her bag up the stairs, to a volley of loud creaks from each step.

Hearing the master bedroom door close, it reminded Tyler of the sound he'd heard when he watched the image of Emily - or so it seemed - walking into the master bedroom and closing the door. He knew he should have told her about this experience, but suspected it was just his imagination and nothing to report. He pulled the covers back, and, after changing into his pajamas, crawled into bed. Once warm and cozy, he realized he'd forgotten to close the door, but decided it wouldn't matter too much. He quickly fell asleep due to the exhaustion of excitement, travel and set up.

After a few hours of deep sleep, Tyler was abruptly jolted awake by a loud beeping sound coming from one of his REM pods - the ghost hunters' name for the stuffy sounding "radiating electro-magneticity devices." He sat straight up in bed and grabbed his iPhone, bringing it close to his face to check the time. It was 2:59 a.m. He chuckled as 3:00 a.m. was supposed to be the bewitching hour, when spirits are said to be at their most powerful.

He always thought of this as a cliché, because if spirits really wanted to show themselves, they would. Why wait till a certain time? Unless residual entities were somehow tied to manifesting or repeating some action at a specific hour.

He crawled out of bed and made his way towards the bedroom door. There was only a very dim light filtering through the windows from the almost full moon. Tyler used his phone to light his way to the switch by the door. Turning on the light, which cast a glow into the lobby, Tyler noticed that the front door had been opened about halfway and was letting in the crisp fall air. But this air was different. It was way, way beyond crisp. Tyler was suddenly shaking with the cold, noticing he could even see his breath rising in little white clouds. But then, just as quickly as he felt the cold, it was gone.

As Tyler reached out to close the door the REM pod went off again, beeping loudly throughout the house. The sound originated from the dining room, where they'd positioned the small cylindrical object, with its twelve-inch antenna sticking straight up. The red power lights were flashing dimly. Tyler walked towards the dining room to check out what might be causing it to go off. As he reached the doorway, he heard Emily's door open.

He could hear the unmistakable sound of footsteps above him on the hardwood floors, followed by the stairs creaking as she - or someone or something - made their way down. He briefly had a flashback to the image he saw while in the library, fervently hoping that what was coming down the stairs was truly Emily. He spotted a small bobbing light coming his way. "Emily is that you?", he called out, his voice rising with trepidation. To his relief she replied: "Yeah! What's going on down here?" while waving her phone around. That explained the tiny bobbing light, then.

"I'm not sure. The REM pod started going off and woke me up. When I got to the hallway, the front door was open, so I closed it. Then it started going off again." Tyler looked at the REM pod as it sat on the dining room table beeping loudly, its red-light flashing. He added, "Now it's just going off like crazy, and I can't think why."

Emily arrived by his side, commenting with some satisfaction: "Well, this is an exciting first night! I was pretty sure we locked that front door before we went to bed. We did, didn't we?"

"Yeah, I thought so too," he replied.

But then, just as abruptly as the beeping had started, it stopped. There was complete silence in the house. Emily and Tyler stood in the doorway of the dining room watching the REM pod intently, breathing hard and wondering if it was going to start up again. Shining her phone light into the kitchen, Emily grabbed one of the digital voice recorders from the counter and turned it on. She checked the time on her phone and raised the recording device up to her mouth. "Tuesday, October twenty-sixth, 3:15 a.m., Dining Room," she said, placing the device on the table next to the REM pod. She made sure that it wasn't going to set the REM pod off, then spoke into it again, in her special, calm investigator's voice, aiming for neutrality:

"Hello. My name is Emily, and this is my friend Tyler. We are going to be staying here with you for the week. We just wanted to introduce ourselves and let you know that you are welcome to communicate with us if you would like."

"Yes, please feel free to communicate with us," Tyler said, "We have a device here on the table with a blue light. If we are not able to hear you now, we may be able to hear you when we play the recording back in the morning."

"Can you tell us your name?" Emily asked. They waited in silence for a few moments before asking the next question, giving whoever or whatever the chance to respond.

"Can you tell us what year it is?" Tyler asked. After a few moments he followed up with, "Was it you that opened the front door?"

They continued to bounce questions back and forth for the next fifteen minutes or so but received nothing audible in response. They left the recorder on in case any entity decided to communicate throughout the rest of the night. They examined the front door but noticed nothing that would explain it opening by itself. They closed it, securing the deadbolt, hoping this would keep it closed, though they were sure they had done this prior to going to sleep. Emily headed back upstairs, and Tyler made his way back to his room. He heard the door to the upstairs bedroom close as he was lying back down. There was an uneasy feeling in the pit of his stomach that something just wasn't right about this house, but he couldn't put his finger on what was causing this unease. He closed his eyes and tried to go back to sleep though he wasn't sure he would be able to do so.

Day Two

Tuesday October 26, 2021

Tyler awoke the next morning to the sound of dishes clanging and the smell of fresh coffee brewing. He grabbed his phone and made his way to the kitchen. Over by the stove stood Emily, who looked like she was struggling with a large electric skillet bubbling with heaped eggs and bacon. The smell filled the room - he could almost taste the deliciously salty meat.

"Good morning!" he said. "What's all this? I didn't know you brought actual food supplies."

"Actually, I didn't. I couldn't really get back to sleep, so after tossing and turning for about three hours, I decided to get up and run to the grocery store. I'm surprised I didn't wake you."

"I must have been completely knocked out. Thanks so much for this though. It smells amazing," Tyler said, grabbing a mug from a cabinet and pouring himself a cup of coffee. He placed his cup on the island next to the DVR, but before sitting down, picked up the recorder they had left on the table earlier that morning. "This is Tyler. Ending recording session of the dining room at 9:17 a.m., October twenty-sixth," he said into the recorder and pressed the stop button. Back in the kitchen, he sat down on a bar stool near the DVR System.

"I figured we were going to need some nourishment to get us up to speed with last night's footage. I really want to check out the door opening business," Emily said, passing Tyler his plate of double eggs and bacon. "Here you go."

"True dat!" Tyler said, looking around for a fork. He nearly fell off the bar stool spinning round to reach the cutlery drawer.

"Here let me," Emily said, jumping in to help. "It's

too early in the morning for a death by bar stool scene. Can't be joining the ghost just yet."

Tyler laughed and replied, "Definitely not!"

As they ate breakfast, they discussed how to break down the day to maximize their time. They decided that they would spend the first few hours of the morning reviewing the cameras and audio from the night. Tyler would review the audio recorder, while Emily would focus on the surveillance footage. Once the audio was completed, they could both review the cameras since the DVR would show all of them on one screen.

Tyler plugged the digital recorder into his computer, transferring the file from last night into his audio program, which he would use to review, cut or amplify anything that might stand out or was in any way anomalous. He placed the noise canceling headphones over his ears and began listening, remembering the brief series of events of the night before, the questions that arose, and their decision to call it a night and head back to sleep. Nothing immediately stood out while listening. The results weren't promising, with nil responses to any of their questions. He could dimly hear their distant conversations about the door opening, and the two of them verifying it was now securely locked. He barely heard Emily's bedroom door closing as she went back to bed. After this, there was dead silence except for the hiss of the recorder.

About an hour in, he pricked up his ears: there appeared to be a distant conversation taking place. He listened intently, trying to make out what was being said. He nudged Emily, while he was listening to indicate he might actually have something. The mystery conversation appeared to go on for a good minute or so and sounded as if an older woman and a gentleman were having a heated argument over something, but he couldn't make out their words. He passed the earphones to Emily, but she couldn't make out any words either, but they'd definitely picked up something - which sounded like it may have come from the kitchen area. Tyler decided to create a clip of the audio file so that he could try to amplify the sound. Frustratingly, however, the amplification failed to clarify the scenario, distorting the conversation even further. He named the clip "EVP 1 - Dining Room" for Electronic Voice Phenomenon, carefully moving it to a folder he created for that day. He continued listening but nothing else seemed to appear on the audio. After completing the audio review, he rejoined Emily who was still reviewing the DVR screens.

"Did you get to the point of the door opening yet?" he asked.

"Not yet. I wanted to review that with you since you actually witnessed it," she replied.

They pulled up the relevant camera on the screen and set it to view at three times the normal speed so they wouldn't be sitting there all day. The camera had been positioned at the top of the stairs and was pointing down directly into the foyer area. It covered the entire entryway, including a full view of the front door. They watched themselves set up the camera and then move on to others while it recorded an empty foyer. An hour or so later, according to the video timestamp, they saw themselves come in, check the door locks and go their separate ways to bed. Tyler went into his room off the lobby and Emily disappeared up the stairs. There was no other movement in the foyer until about 2:50 a.m. when the front door slowly opened on its own. Hardly able to breathe, they used the DVR's zoom to try and get a better view of the deadbolt and doorknob to see if they could see them turn. That would be particularly interesting - to say the least! - as the footage had just shown them definitely locking it. Staring, fascinated at the screen, there it was… they could actually see the door unlocking itself as if someone was using a key from the outside - except, of course, no one was… About ten minutes later, Tyler's bedroom light came on and he made an appearance in the foyer.

"What are you doing?" Emily asked.

"I was trying to see if I could really see my breath. It was so cold, but was it just the door being open, or… well… some kind of a spirit making the temperature drop by taking my energy to try and materialize? They say that happens at haunted sites…" Tyler said. "But in any case, it went away as quickly as it came."

They continued to watch Tyler close the door and

then head off out of sight down the hall to where the REM pod had been going off. A few minutes later Emily's head appeared as she was walking down the stairs and made her way into the dining room. There was no other activity with the door for the rest of the night until Emily left to go out later that morning.

Tyler suggested that they watch some video footage from around the time of the EVP that cropped up on the digital recorder. He figured it would have been around 4:30 a.m. so they queued up all the video screens onto the monitor and started the playback just before then. They watched the monitors closely, reviewing a few hours of the footage to see if anything out of the ordinary happened, but unfortunately, there was nothing.

Being well past noon, they decided to shower and get dressed. The plan was to head into town and visit the local library to check out any information related to the property. If they could dig up the names of the former owners or even those who died in car accidents along the curve, this would give them something solid to draw on during their investigation that night. Their hearty breakfast would have to carry them through until the evening.

While Emily took the lead on showering, Tyler spent the time upstairs in the library browsing through the bookcases along the walls, filled mostly with leather-bound old books. The lettering of their titles was so badly faded as to be barely readable. Glass doors must have been installed to help protect what was left of these old books and documents. As he was running his finger across one of the rows, he noticed an unusual book - very different from all the others on this shelf. It was a large binder like tome, almost like a modern-day scrapbook. It barely fit on the shelf, pushing at the glass front. Tyler pulled it down, taking a seat in anticipation of a good read. But as he opened it a handful of newspaper clippings fell out. Retrieving them from the floor, he began to carefully flip through them, noticing that each was about a different accident that had occurred in front of the house.

Andrew Jennings Dead in Head on Collision

Carol Ann Mathis Killed Along Dead Man's Curve

Jeremy Wheeler (16) Killed In 3 Car Accident

Tyler counted ten clippings that he'd picked up but there were still more tucked inside the book, which were glued and taped to the pages like a memorial photo album for those who had died. But as Tyler examined the articles, he also discovered that not only were their deaths mentioned but there were pages upon pages of clippings that provided information regarding other landmarks in these individuals' lives. Almost as if someone had been keeping track of them. "Kinda stalkerish," Tyler thought to himself as he continued to flip through.

Andrew Jennings Graduates with Honors

Miss Mathis to Wed Mr. Jennings in December Wedding

"Oh, now that's interesting. Two of the people listed in these articles were actually engaged…" Tyler said out loud, though there was no one in the room to hear him. He continued to read, discovering that all three accidents had happened on the same night - 26th October 1961. One of the articles from the front page of the Statesville Record and Landmark went on to say:

3 Dead in Horrible Accident

"Andrew Jennings and his Fiancée, Carol Ann Mathis, were driving along Dead Man's Curve when Mr. Jennings drove too fast and lost control of his car. Miss Mathis was sitting in the car behind him. Her fiancé's car crashed head on into a large oak tree, killing him instantly. Miss Mathis pulled off to the side of the road and ran to the old farmhouse for help, but it appeared no one was home. She was trying to flag down an approaching car, when she stepped too far out into the road and was hit by an on-coming vehicle driven by 16-year-old Jeremy Wheeler. She was also killed instantly. Mr.

Wheeler slammed on his brakes, lost control and crashed sideways into Miss Mathis' car parked on the side of the road. A freight truck and trailer, following behind Mr. Wheeler, then proceeded to t-bone the sideways car. Mr. Jennings, Miss Mathis and Mr. Wheeler were all pronounced dead at the scene."

"Holy shit!" Tyler exclaimed. Emily heard him as she was coming out of the bathroom and poked her head into the library.

"What's that? Why do you look like you've just seen a ghost? *Have* you?" Emily asked, only half-jokingly, as she briskly dried her hair with a towel she'd just unwound from her head. Tyler proceeded to tell her about the book, the newspaper clippings that had fallen out, and the articles that chronicled the lives of the three individuals involved in the accident. Trying to keep his voice steady, he casually added his piece de resistance - today was its sixtieth anniversary.

"You're kidding, right?" Emily said, looking across

at him sharply. Now he'd really gotten her attention.

"Nope! Not in the least. And it happened right in front of this house. Apparently, Carol Ann Mathis ran all the way up here for help, but no one answered the door." Tyler showed Emily the clipping as evidence. "I definitely want to look more into this when we go into town today. I'm gonna bring this book with us, too. It might give us some leads as to which direction to head. I wonder if Carol Ann is…well… who opened the door last night…" Tyler pondered aloud, trailing off. Now he'd actually said it, suddenly the paranormal leapt into sharp focus. If ever ghost hunting had been a game, it wasn't any longer. There was a brief silence as if the gravity of the matter hung heavily between them.

"Hmm, that's an interesting theory." Emily said, "Maybe we can try to find out more on this tonight when we do our EVP sessions. We could even do one in the front yard. Right now, though, you'd better get in the shower so that we can make it into town before places close."

Tyler placed the clippings back inside the book, left

it on a chair and went downstairs to get his change of clothes ready. While he showered, Emily grabbed another cup of coffee and sat out on the front porch watching the traffic hurtle by. She wondered how much fun it would be, trying to get out into the traffic from a concealed entrance on a busy day like this. She also thought about the story that Tyler had just told her - how tragic that a loving couple and a teenager perished on this road, right in front of where she was sitting, sixty years ago. Exactly.

Having safely negotiated his exit from the drive, Tyler arrived at the parking lot of the Statesville Library. It was a rundown building - still with a 1960's or 70's vibe to it - made of brick and trimmed with pebble stone and mortar. Large windows allowed the casual walker to see the library's carefully organized rows of books. As they reached the double door entrance, Tyler did a quick check that none of the articles had fallen out of the book again.

Emily approached the front counter where an older lady was sitting, staring at a computer screen with her bifocals pulled down to the tip of her pale nose. Her gray curls, no doubt freshly permed, were so tight they resembled a football helmet. She wore a white blouse under a red hand-knitted sweater vest. She appeared to be so totally focused on her task - whatever it was - that Emily thought she was being ignored the first time she said hello. The librarian, whose name tag said Sharon, looked up from the computer screen, saying brightly: "Oh, hello there, dear. What can I help you with?" But then Sharon got up and walked over to a printer mumbling something bad-temperedly under her breath about how modern technology was not the greatest thing in the world.

"Hi there." Emily said, "We're here doing some research on a property we are currently staying in for the week. I understand there have been a lot of - "

"Don't tell me - you must be staying in the old Nichols' house out off Dead Man's Curve," Sharon interrupted as she returned to the detested computer.

"You're not the first one to come in here about that place. Probably won't be the last either until they tear that place down."

"Tear it down?" Tyler queried, "Why would anyone want to tear it down?"

"I don't know. I just work here." Sharon snarked back, her initial attempt at civility already a thing of the past. "But I will tell you that you're gonna have a hard time finding any information on that place. Most of it has been lost or is still on old microfiche film that's never been converted to digital. If you ask me, that's the better way to search for things, though it's time consuming."

"We're fine going through microfiche. We're here for the whole week so, if we can't get through everything today, we can always come back." Emily said.

"Hmmmph. Well, we're closed on Wednesdays, and we close at 3 p.m. on Fridays. You know, labor shortages and what not. If you want to use the microfiche, you'll have to share as we only have one machine left. Took all the rest of them out about fifteen years ago when they started converting everything over to - well, you know, these computer systems." Sharon said as she was leading - or more accurately directing - them over toward the microfiche machine. "Any particular time period you are looking for?"

"October 1961, please." Tyler spoke out quickly.

"Ah, yes," Sharon said with a slight smirk, "That's a favorite with all you visiting researchers. I bet you're out there looking for their ghosts, aren't ya?"

"Well, yes, ma'am. Not necessarily their ghosts, but we are paranormal investigators." Emily replied quickly with a sharp hint of attitude, as experience had taught her people tended to ridicule those interested in the paranormal. And she didn't like condescending old ladies who thought they knew what was best for everyone. "We like to compare and back up our findings with research from the area."

"Hhmmph. All a bunch of phooey if you ask me," Sharon snipped back quickly. "Everyone knows the good Lord Jesus takes everyone to Heaven, and if he doesn't, well they don't stay here. They go to the fiery place down below."

"Well, we didn't. Ask you, that is," Emily snarked back, beginning to feel a flush of anger rising up in her neck. "Can you please get us the information we need? And we'll leave you be."

Sharon looked both of them up and down, gave them another "hhmmph", and turned to walk towards the back. Her white Reebok Classics poked out of her droopy brown skirt as she scuffled to a back room. A few minutes later she returned with a reel of film that she hooked to the microfiche machine. Sharon maneuvered the film under a flat glass screen illuminated with light and a microscope pointing down over it. Once secured in place, she flipped the large switch on the front to power the machine - lighting up the sizeable screen.

"Here you go. Just turn the knob right here to go through the reel. Just be careful with it. It can be a little stubborn sometimes," Sharon advised, dangerously close to actually being helpful, before returning to her desk. Emily sat down in front of the machine, staring confusedly at the dinosaur of a computer screen.

"I haven't used one of these in forever," she

commented, gradually turning the knob as the first negative slid across the large white screen.

"I think, if you turn these two little knobs on the front of the screen, it will adjust the focus and contrast in order to make it more readable," Tyler said, pulling up a chair, so that he wasn't constantly leaning over Emily's shoulder. After a few tries they were able to get everything adjusted so that the images could clearly be read. Turning the navigating knob, they began scrolling through image after image of newspaper articles for the month of October 1961. After scrolling for what seemed like hours - though it had only been about thirty minutes - the articles that covered the accident finally appeared. All the articles repeated the story they already knew, except for one that added a few details about where the dead were laid to rest.

"Hey! This says that all three victims were buried in a local church cemetery," Emily said. "Apparently it was Rose Hill Methodist Church, and I think I know where it is."

"Yeah?"

"Yeah. I think I passed it on the way to the store this morning. It kinda sits up on a hill, a little back from the road," Emily responded. "We still have a couple hours before the sun sets. I feel like we should go and pay our respects before we start our investigation tonight."

"That sounds like a really great idea." Tyler agreed.

Emily finished rolling out the rest of the microfiche tape. Once done, She and Tyler made their way back to the front where Sharon was nose deep into her computer screen yet again. Emily, not wanting to disturb her too much, put the reel firmly down in front of her, saying simply, "Thank you." Sharon looked up to make the briefest possible eye contact with her, as if saying "you're welcome" was too much trouble. Not wanting to deal with her anymore that day, they left.

Starting the car, they noticed it was a little after four o'clock in the afternoon, and the sun was about to set in about an hour. If they wanted to make it to the cemetery before dark, they should get a move on. They searched the GPS for Rose Hill Methodist Church and tapped go when the directions came up. It only took them about twenty minutes to make the drive across town, and, as they turned up the hill and into the parking lot, they spotted the graveyard to the right of the church. Tyler pulled the car up to the verge of the grass and put it in park. The parking lot was empty, and the redbrick church had a distinctly eerie feel to it. The grass in the cemetery was a bit overgrown, like they had forgotten to give it the last cut of the season and leaves were starting to cover some of the flat grave markers. They got out of the car and realized that there were more graves than they had initially thought. The graveyard extended down the hill that ended close to the highway.

Deciding they could cover more ground if they split up, Tyler took the bottom of the hill near the road with Emily at the back near the tree line. They walked each row reading the names on every stone, searching for Carol, Andrew or Jeremy.

Tyler came across a group of stones with the last name Wheeler - just peering at them - when his foot accidentally brushed some leaves away, uncovering a near deteriorated plaque in the ground. He bent down to brush all the leaves away so that he could see it more clearly. The plaque was there to mark the grave of someone without a stone marker. Though the card inside the marker had all but faded away, he was still able to make out a W and assumed it went along with the rest of the nearby Wheelers. There wasn't any visible indication that the grave belonged to Jeremy, though his intuition told him it did. After closing his eyes briefly in respect, he continued along the row of stones.

Emily, on the other hand, was having no such luck at locating any of the three last names. However, she found quite a few Nichols' stones. One that seemed to stand out to her was a large black rectangular stone bearing the name across the top. On the left was the name William Nichols, and below that were the dates April 7, 1857 - October 31, 1929. To his right was Mary Nichols and the dates below read July 15, 1875 - October 31, 1952. Emily immediately noticed that they died on the same day- Halloween - but twenty-three years apart. She wondered if they were related to the Nichols who owned the house they were investigating. She took a picture of the stone with her phone, so that they could look into it properly later, and moved on along the rows.

The sun was nearly gone when Tyler came across Andrew Jennings' gravestone, in the center of the cemetery, with the words "Gone too soon, but not forgotten" incised across the top. There were a few other Jennings scattered around close by but no signs of Carol Ann Mathis anywhere. By the dates on the stone, Tyler could see that Andrew had been born on August 8, 1936, and was only twenty-five when the tragic accident had occurred. He knelt down to the grave, brushed the fallen leaves away from the base of the stone, and closed his eyes to take a brief moment of silence to pay his respects. When Tyler opened his eyes and looked up he spotted Emily kneeling over a flat grave marker in the ground. Standing up, he patted Andrew's stone and made his way over to Emily, who was on the west end of the cemetery.

"I found Andrew over there," he said, pointing, "Is this Carol?"

"Yeah. She was only 23. How sad is that?" Emily replied.

"I know. Andrew was only 25." Tyler knelt down beside Emily, who was clearly welling up, deeply moved, though - being her - she was fighting hard not to show it.

"Did you find Jeremy?" Emily asked.

"I think so. Though I'm not one hundred percent sure it's him. There's no actual stone. Just a marker," Tyler answered.

"Wow. That's so sad - if it is him." Emily said, picking a dandelion from the tall grass and laying it on Carol's stone. "The sun's nearly gone. We should probably go find something for dinner and get back to the house. Hopefully, the driveway is easier to find in the dark now that we know what to expect."

"Yeah, really," Tyler said as they stood up to make their way back to the car. They both closed their eyes one more time, but this time they invited Carol, Andrew and Jeremy to visit them tonight, though careful not to invite anyone or anything else along for the ride. Once back in the car, they pulled up Google to locate a place to grab something for dinner. Suddenly food was very important

- it dawned on them they'd skipped lunch. It seems most likely eateries were ten minutes back into town so they headed in that direction.

They settled on a local pizzeria. It was a welcome opportunity to kick back and really relax, and finally get to eat something. It had already been a long day, and much more was still to come... In the fuzzy glow that too much pizza gives, they contentedly went over their findings in the graveyard, comparing notes on their agenda for the night. Tyler made sure to be extra careful as he approached the driveway, and to his - and Emily's - enormous relief, he was able to navigate it much easier than the night before. Going up the driveway, for a brief moment they noticed what appeared to be a flickering candlelight in an upstairs window - Emily's room. Chalking it up to the reflection of their headlights, they agreed they should have left a light on for when they returned. As they parked and turned the headlights off, everything was engulfed by a deep, deadening darkness.

Night Two

Tuesday October 26, 2021

Emily and Tyler decided to start their investigation outside on the front lawn. Tyler hooked up an infrared (IR) light attachment to a mini digital camcorder and set it up on a tripod facing towards the tricky curve in the road. The IR light would allow the camcorder to see in the dark, enhancing its night vision function. The glow from the IR's red light in the almost total darkness produced a distinctly creepy feeling, especially when their faces were thrown into weird, crimson shadows. While they'd left lights on downstairs, they had agreed to turn the porch light off.

It was around ten-thirty when they finally finished

setting up chairs, camera, digital voice recorders, and wiring to their satisfaction. Tyler hoped that the traffic wouldn't cause their equipment to vibrate too much or distort any audio recordings. Emily had grabbed a couple of the fold-up chairs she always carried in her trunk and positioned them to face the highway. Now whatever happened would happen. They both took deep breaths, trying to stay emotionally neutral and professionally objective, and not to anticipate any particular outcome - especially a dramatic one.

They began the investigation with an EVP session. Tyler turned on the digital voice recorder and placed it on a notepad on the ground between them.

"Hello, my name is Emily."

"And I'm Tyler."

"We're here tonight to get to know you. To hear your story. We are not here to harm you, only to talk with you." Emily announced, before pausing briefly, waiting for a response. The lack of night-time traffic whooshing past them made time seem to stand still.

"Andrew? Carol? Jeremy? Are any of you here with

us tonight?" Tyler asked. "We know tonight is the sixtieth anniversary of your death, and we would love to hear from you on what actually happened that night in 1961."

Emily turned to Tyler, murmuring: "Might not be too smart to mention their passing. After all, they might not even realize that's what happened to them."

Tyler was embarrassed by his rookie mistake. All proper investigators knew that some spirits, especially those who died unexpectedly or violently - such as in a car accident - are left disembodied and confused, not being aware they'd passed. It wasn't just a breach of protocol he'd just committed, nor simply bad manners, but he could even have set the whole investigation back. The spirits might take offense or fright and that would be the end of their week. And his reputation would be gone. He quickly apologized to Emily and the spirits if they could hear him. The last thing he wanted was to piss off the very souls they were there to contact. It seemed Emily was in a forgiving mood, but there was still another moment of silence before she went on.

"Can you tell us what year it is? Or can you tell us your name?"

Silence.

Tyler saw a flash of light out of the corner of his left eye and immediately turned to look. By the time he'd screwed his neck as far round as he could to the left, nothing was in sight. But then came a car traveling towards the curve, its lights reflecting off the trees, creating a fiery illusion of crape myrtles. He figured whatever he'd seen was just a reflection.

"Car," he announced, to tag the sound on the recorder for future reference.

As the silence enveloped them again Emily asked, "Andrew, I hear you are getting married. Are you excited? Is Carol excited?"

Silence.

"Andrew, the people who once owned this house kept some newspaper clippings of you in their library. Did you know these people?" Tyler asked.

Silence. Disappointing. But that's paranormal research for you. You have to have the patience - and hope - of a saint.

After about forty to forty-five minutes of questions, they decided to end the EVP session, but left the digital recorder on to capture anything that may want to communicate throughout the night. Emily suggested that they try using the Phasma Box and pulled out her laptop and external speaker, balancing the former on a chair arm.

"What exactly is the Phasma Box? How does it work?" Tyler asked, "I've heard of it before, but haven't been around when it's actually being used."

"It's a Windows-based program that gives the spirits a way to communicate with or answer us by manipulating sound waves. It has an in-built word bank that allegedly the spirits can manipulate to converse with us, though some of the things I've heard come through, I don't think you'd ever find in any respectable word bank," Emily grinned, adding, "The program has similar features to what some refer to as a spirit box or portal."

"Oh ok. That sounds like fun. Sure, let's give it a try." Tyler responded Emily opened the program and clicked the start button. Immediately strange sounds started coming from the external speaker. They sounded like words, but the reverb created an echo. The sound reminded Tyler of when he was a kid and used to talk through the oscillating fan his mother had in the living room. Distorted and weird - though of course not actually ghostly.

They reintroduced themselves for the start of the Phasma Box session and began asking questions to the empty air.

"Is anyone with us tonight?" Emily asked.

Multiple echoes poured from the speaker. But - wait - one sounded very much like a "Yes".

"Can you tell us your name?" Tyler asked.

More echoes came tumbling out, sounding like multiple voices all trying to talk at once, though try as they might, they couldn't hear a single obvious name.

"Can you tell us what happened here on this night sixty years ago?" Tyler asked.

For a moment there was very little noise from the speaker. Then out of nowhere they were hit by an appalling cacophony of squealing brakes. Just when they thought they could bear it no longer, it was replaced by a loud crash that reverberated through their heads. Fearing for their eardrums, they pushed their hands against their ears, but the hellish metallic sound seemed to go on and on… but then came siren after siren from emergency vehicles that blurred into one hideous throbbing wail… The sirens stopped. Just as Tyler and Emily were exchanging stunned glances and taking their hands from their ears, they were frozen by what sounded like a gunshot. A single, loud gunshot. Then the speaker fell silent.

They sat stunned for a few long moments, hearts thudding wildly. When Tyler spoke, he found himself inanely stating the obvious: "Whoa! That was the sound of an accident - well, maybe even *the* accident - as it actually happened!" His voice shook with awe and excitement.

Emily was obviously made of sterner stuff - or more experienced. Or just better at containing it. She said in a studiedly normal tone: "Yeah, that's very interesting. I've never heard it do that before. Normally, it's just super creepy echoes and the occasional words. And was that a gunshot at the end? I swear it was. But I don't remember hearing anything about anyone being shot out here."

"I think we should continue asking more questions. We may get to the bottom of this after all," Tyler declared.

They duly asked question after question - attempting to validate what they had just experienced - hoping the computer program would deliver the answers they wanted, but the few responses they did receive were mainly gibberish. There were a few random "Hi's" and "Hellos" apparently from various voices, but nothing that responded further or pertained to their questions. By this time it was close to two in the morning, and Tyler and Emily were starting to feel drained of all energy. They decided to call it quits for the night.

As they started to pack up, and as he was disassembling the camcorder, he turned to get one last shot of the house. Looking through the small LCD screen on the camera as he panned around, he noticed a figure in Emily's bedroom moving across the lighted doorway through one of the windows. He started to point it out, but realized Emily was nowhere around. She must have taken the chairs inside the house. Unfortunately, until he could catch up with her and check her whereabouts, he would have to disregard it. He could always take a better look at the video at their morning evidence review.

It didn't take long to move all their stuff back into the house. Both of them sat down gratefully in the kitchen to make the most of a late-night snack of potato chips and bottled water before heading to bed.

"That was amazing!" Tyler declared, "I've never had an experience like that."

"It's why I love using the Phasma Box. You never know what to expect," Emily said.

Tyler began setting the equipment up in the order he would process it in the morning. "I think we should start with the audio recorder first. This way we can check for EVPs and see if the sounds of the accident were caught."

"It should be on there," Emily commented, brushing slivers of chips off her lap, "It certainly was loud enough. I'm surprised the neighbors didn't hear it."

"I don't think we are that close to the people in the area," Tyler remarked, "There's quite a bit of land out there between houses."

He took this time to bring up what he'd seen while breaking down the camera. "Hey, I just wanted to flag up - maybe for the log - that, when I was taking down the camera, I panned around to the front of the house and got a shot of you upstairs in the bedroom."

"Really? I brought the chairs and a few other things into the house while we were packing up, but I didn't go upstairs. Let me see that camera - I think we need to review this before even thinking of going to bed." Emily's sudden and obvious urgency seemed like an unspoken reproof: "Idiot - you should have pointed it out much earlier!". But still she said nothing.

Swallowing down his embarrassment, Tyler handed the camera over to Emily who plugged it into the laptop, calling up the video footage onto the screen. Skipping to the end where Tyler was taking down the camera, they could see it pan round for a full view of the house. They could clearly see the doorway through the bedroom windows - illuminated by the light filtering into the hallway. There in the deepest, darkest shadows a dark image emerged and moved across the room, blocking out all visible light.

"That's not me!" Emily exclaimed. "We need to go upstairs and make sure there isn't someone in this house before we try to sleep."

"Soooo… there's something else I haven't told you." Tyler said, hesitantly, shuffling his feet. "I didn't really think anything of it until now, but last night, while we were setting up the equipment, I was in the library and saw someone walk down the hall and into this very bedroom. They just walked in and closed the door. I thought it was you, but then again it didn't really look like you, so I dismissed it as imagination or something. I walkie'd you, and you were downstairs… So yeah… I…" Tyler's nervous rambling ground to a halt.

"Wait a minute. You've seen this person before and didn't even think to tell me?" Emily interrupted. "Tyler, you know you're supposed to make me aware of anything you might think you've seen for us to properly investigate and - if it's easily explained away - to debunk."

"I'm sorry. I just..." Tyler said, standing there, a picture of embarrassed remorse.

There was a loaded pause, but then she said forcibly, "It's fine. Let's just see if we can get a better look at this image. I think if we screenshot it we can use a photo editing program to blow up or zoom in on the figure in the background."

As Tyler had no other solution, she went ahead with her plan. He moved around behind her so that he could get a better view of the computer screen. While the zoomed-in image was dark and pixelated, it was easier to see that there was a glimmer of candlelight illuminating a face... Tyler could feel the excited tension rising between them as they stared hard at the screen. There really was a face - and it seemed to belong to an older woman. Where the candlelight was coming from was a mystery, as there were no lit candles in any rooms in the house. They knew there were old stories of an old lady's ghost roaming around - but was this actually her, right there on their computer screen?

"Look at this - you can see distinct features. You can make out the jawline and nose. The eyes seem to be sunken just a bit," Emily pointed out.

"There's a strong resemblance to the Wicked Witch of the West from the Wizard of Oz. You know, just minus the hat and the garb," Tyler said.

"Yeah, I can see that, I guess," Emily replied, with a certain remoteness in her voice perhaps, to signal she wasn't seeing whatever Tyler saw - or at least she wasn't going to play ball with his Wizard of Oz flippancy - and anyway she was still frustrated with him. "Ok, well, I think we need to grab a recorder, a camera, maybe even the dowsing rods and go investigate this room. I'm not sure I want to sleep in there tonight unless we do. We should also do a complete walkthrough to rule out that there's no one else in this house besides the two of us. We also need to make a note to review the DVR footage in the morning. We may be able to get a better image of this old lady."

Before going upstairs, they made a complete

walkthrough of the first floor to rule out any uninvited visitors being downstairs. While trying to get back on Emily's good side, Tyler repeated his quick Harry Potter joke while looking in the cabinet under the staircase. Unfortunately, she just stared at him as if she could have locked him in there herself. Ok, no more Harry Potter and no more Wizard of Oz. This was one very intensely focused lady. The awkwardness continued as they gathered as much equipment as they could carry and made their way up the stairs.

The two split up, checking each of the rooms and closets to make sure no one was there. They then met up in the bedroom and looked for a source of light that would explain the apparent candlelight reflection on the woman's face. They made sure that everything was just as it was when the camera had panned across the front windows, turning out all the upstairs lights. However, the bathroom light remained on.

Emily sat down on the floor in front of the fireplace. She was holding a dowsing rod in each hand that she adjusted to point straight out into the room, while Tyler had opted to operate the video camera and record the dowsing rod session. He lay down on the floor just in front of the bed and held the camera up.

"So, how are these supposed to work again?" Tyler had to ask, though he reckoned after that it would be best to stay quiet as possible for the rest of the night.

Emily, still annoyed with him, briefly replied, with a sharp edge in her voice: "Dowsing rods were originally used back in the day for people to find water - water divining, it was called. The idea was that, tapping into the operator's own energy and unconscious knowledge, the rods would point in the direction of the water source. But for us, just as with any of our equipment, they are just another way for spirits to communicate. You can ask them to cross the bars for "yes" or keep them in a neutral position for "no." Ensuring the metal rods were parallel, she began to ask questions.

"Hello. My name is Emily, and this is Tyler. We think we may have seen you from outside. If that was you, can you please cross the rods for yes?"

Tyler focused the camera more so that any

movement would be visible on the playback. He was fascinated to see that the rods did in fact begin to move, each one turning in towards the other until they had created a near perfect X.

"Thank you," Emily said. "Can you please move the rods back where they were?"

The metal arms remained in the X position for some time before gradually moving back to the straight position.

"Did this used to be your house?" Emily asked, "Cross the rods for yes, please."

The rods quickly swung back into an X.

"Thank you. Can you put them back, please?"

The rods moved back to where they had started. When they had reached the straight position, Emily began her next question:

"Was it you that Tyler saw a couple days ago while he was setting up the camera? Cross the rods for yes, please."

The rods stayed in the straight position.

"OK. Thank you," Emily said. "Are there more than

one of you here with us then? Cross the rods for yes."

The rods quickly swung into the X position.

"Thank you. Can you please move them back?"

This time, instead of returning to the neutral position, the metal arms began to swing towards Tyler. The left rod pointed directly at him with the tip of the right oscillating to touch the left - forming a perfect forty-five-degree angle that speared at his face.

"Interesting. Is there something you want to say to Tyler? Cross the rods for yes, please?"

The rods did not cross for yes, but instead did a near-complete 180 degree and swung sharply inwards towards Emily herself, knocking against her arms as they did so.

"Is there something you would like to say to me? Cross the rods for yes, please."

The rods didn't budge.

"OK. I am going to reset the rods and we can start again," Emily said, shaking out her arms to loosen them up, and repositioning the rods to point forward again. "I am sleeping in this room during our stay here. Is it safe to stay in this room? Please cross the rods for yes."

The rods remained utterly still, but during the heavily anticipatory silence, faint clanging could be heard coming from the kitchen below. It sounded as if someone was either washing the dishes or putting clean ones away. There was the sound of conversation, though no actual words could be made out. Tyler lifted his head up from the floor, where he had almost fallen asleep, considering it was four in the morning. He and Emily locked eyes in the gloomy bedroom - and as one, they immediately jumped up and ran down to the kitchen. Nothing appeared to have been moved, and there wasn't anyone in there but themselves.

"Something is starting to be *really* strange about this place," Emily said, her voice slightly too firm. Was she actually trying to conceal some real fear? Clearing her throat, she added, "I could have sworn we just heard someone in this kitchen."

"You could hear things moving and people talking," Tyler nodded.

"Well, it's about 4:15 now. I think we need to try

and get some rest. Otherwise, we're not going to be in a fit state for any research tomorrow. I'm definitely not sleeping in that room tonight. I think I'll crash on the couch in the living room, but not in that room," Emily said, heading to the living room.

"You could sleep in my room, and I can take the sofa if you would like." Tyler said, still not sure if she was upset with him.

"No. It's fine. I can sleep in here. I think there are supposed to be blankets in this closet," she added.

Emily opened the closet door to find an old wood trunk. She figured the blankets were stored there so she tried to open it, but it wouldn't budge. It appeared to be stuck or locked. She wrestled with it for a bit - trying to get it open - but quickly gave up as exhaustion began to set in. Grabbing a throw pillow from a chair, she collapsed exhaustedly onto the couch. Tyler wasn't sure what was going on, but when he realized that there weren't any blankets to be had, he went into his room and grabbed the bedspread. He laid it gently over Emily's curled up body.

Feeling a bit of remorse for his rookie mistakes he timidly whispered, "I'm sorry," before turning off the light. Back in his own room, he closed the door to give them both some privacy and pulled the sheet back from the neatly made-up bed - as in, come to think of it, the mysteriously, neatly made-up bed… He didn't recall making it that morning, and he hadn't noticed when he grabbed the bedspread for Emily. But if he didn't make the bed, then who did? While it might be useful to have an invisible servant to help with the chores - he really could have done with one at home - even to a ghostbuster it wasn't an entirely welcomed situation… No, not possible, surely. But he would still ask Emily in the morning if she'd had a fit of room-maid activity while he was in the shower. He didn't want to bother her any more tonight and hopefully she wouldn't be as exasperated with him once they had both gotten some sleep.

Day Three

Wednesday October 27, 2021

Most of the day had passed when Tyler awoke. It was almost three in the afternoon and there wasn't a sound from anywhere in the house. Wondering if Emily was awake, he made himself presentable and opened the bedroom door. She wasn't there, the bedspread tossed carelessly over the back of the couch. He made his way into the kitchen and found her sitting at the island with her face buried in her hands.

"Good morning," he said meekly, already aware she was unnerved.

"Good morning," she sighed, raising her head.

"Are you ok? I hope you got some quality rest last night. Again, I'm sorry I didn't tell you about things sooner. I'll do better in the future," Tyler said, head down apologetically.

"It's fine, I'm fine. Thank you for the blanket last night. Let's just put that behind us and focus on the evidence we captured last night," Emily replied. "I made some coffee, though it may not be hot anymore. It's been a while since it was made."

"That's ok. I can make a fresh pot," Tyler said lightly - keen to keep the conversation easy- as he busied himself with the coffee maker.

"I just can't figure out why there's nothing on these surveillance cameras from last night. I know they were on. I know they were recording. It just doesn't make any sense," Emily said, turning her attention once more to working out why the footage would not replay.

"Wait, you mean there's *nothing*? Does it just skip time?" Tyler asked puzzled.

"Pretty much. There's some kind of malfunction or something," Emily said.

"Well, damn. I wanted to use it to review the camera in my room… speaking of… Did you make my bed yesterday while I was in the shower?" he asked, feeling foolish. This was Emily, after all - the last person to have secret room-maid ambitions!

"Umm, no. Of course not! Why would you even ask?" Emily's eyebrows shot up. Fortunately, she was bewildered rather than insulted.

"I didn't notice it when I gave you the bedspread, but when I went to get in the bed, I noticed the sheet was pulled up. Just as if the bed had been made. I'm pretty sure it wasn't me. I'm not a great bed maker. So, obviously… I wondered who might have," Tyler said, pouring himself a fresh cup of coffee. "Like you said last night. This house is starting to get really strange."

"I think we need to go through what evidence we can and organize it into separate categories. We need structure. There's way too much going on here. Car accidents, mysterious old women, possible doppelganger activity - not to mention invisible servants…" she said.

"It might be best if we take a break from investigating

tonight. Most of the day is nearly gone anyways," Tyler suggested. "We can take this time to figure out what happened to the cameras and get all of the audio and camcorders reviewed. We can also start building case files in Word so that we can access them easily."

"That's a great idea. We may need to get a new DVR box if we can't figure out how to get it working again," Emily replied, attempting to restart the DVR system.

"Awesome! I'll start working on compiling Word documents on everything we have while I'm listening to the audio from last night," Tyler remarked briskly over his shoulder as he walked out of the kitchen, priding himself on how efficient he sounded.

Tyler figured that setting up in the dining room would give Emily space to work on the DVR system, and they could still communicate since they were directly across the hall from one another. Once things were settled, he plugged the recorder into the laptop and began transferring the audio files from last night. He opened a blank Word document, while waiting for the transfer to finish, and titled it "The Accident." He did another for "The House," leaving another one blank in case anything else came up during review. The transfer still had a few minutes left when Emily came into the dining room.

"We're going to need a whole new DVR system. I can't for the life of me figure out what is wrong or how to fix it," she commented, running a hand through her mane of blonde hair frustratedly. "At this point it is going to be easier to just get a new one. So, before we head into town for that, I'll take over the camcorders, while you do the audio."

"Cool deal! Thanks!" Tyler replied and passed her the camcorders.

The audio had finished transferring and Tyler donned his noise canceling earphones, securing them tightly to his ears. He started with their EVP session. At the same time, he was typing up everything they'd discovered about the accident of 1961 into the associated Word document. This was one of the perks of reviewing the audio. He didn't have to be completely focused on looking for movement on a screen. He could easily continue working on whatever, while listening to the events that played out the night before. If something strange or out of the ordinary caught his ear, all he had to do was rewind just a little to replay.

The EVP session didn't yield as many results as they had hoped. Actually, there weren't any. It was just as silent after each question as it had been last night in real time. Moving on to the Phasma Box recording, things were a bit more interesting, and took a little more concentration since - rather excitingly - multiple sounds and voices were coming through. For most of it, there was just gibberish, until he reached the point where Emily asked about the accident. It was plain as day that the sounds coming through the speaker box were that of a car accident. As the squealing brakes could be heard much clearer, Tyler assumed it was because the recorder was on the ground in front of the speaker box. The crash was even louder, the dreadful cacophony of metal crumbling and glass shattering making Tyler's whole body cringe, almost as if it were happening to himself. The sirens came blaring through earphones as if they were right inside the room with him. The sound of what they believed had to be a gunshot nearly blew out Tyler's eardrum, but it was what came after that really caught his attention.

Steadying himself with an effort after feeling he'd just suffered a very real ordeal, Tyler flipped down the open apps to get to the audio program and used the mouse to scroll back, oh so gently, on the audio. He pressed the earphones close to his ear, hoping to get an even clearer sound. He braced himself for the loud gunshot - which duly came, dreadful in its starkness - then distinct sound of running footsteps that got louder as they rapidly drew closer to the recorder. Tyler knew that no one was running while they were out there, as both of them were in their chairs balancing Emily's laptop between them, and he was sure they would have noticed even the slightest movement. Tyler duly highlighted the relevant area of audio and created a short clip of the sounds. He then enhanced it by removing the omnipresent hiss that appears on every recording and amplified it so it could be heard without the use of earphones. He listened again.

This time as the footsteps were approaching there was a faint yell in the background - panicky, almost as if someone were shouting for help. Tyler removed the earphones and reached across the table to get Emily's attention.

"You've got to hear this," he said urgently.

He unplugged the earphones from the computer and turned the volume up as far as it would go. Emily listened intently. She too heard the footsteps and the cries for help. Frowning with concentration, she then had him replay the clip.

"Those are distinct footsteps, as if someone was running from the accident," she remarked. "It's just like in the article - Carol, running up to the house for help after Andrew's car had crashed."

"That's exactly what I was thinking," Tyler replied. "This is definitely a good one to keep. How's the video going?

"Nothing eventful yet, but I'm coming up on the same scene, and I'm curious if the same sounds were caught on the camcorder," Emily said.

Tyler went back to listening to his audio, and Emily watched the screen closely for anything that would stand out as paranormal, her own earphones also clamped tightly to her head with slightly sweaty palms. As the sounds of the accident were coming through the speaker, she could see their own white, intensely focused faces on the screen. When the sound of the gunshot went off, the camera on the screen flashed with a white light that faded back into normal view. The sounds of the footsteps were simply not there - though those heartrending cries for help were. But there was a new horror… the cries had been bad enough before, but now it sounded for all the world as if it was *Emily* crying for help….

"Watch this!" she exclaimed excitedly, rewinding the video.

Tyler watched and listened as the white light appeared on the screen, then came the sounds of that harrowing cry for help. He looked up at Emily in pure amazement. He wasn't sure what to make of what he'd just heard. He knew that no one else was out there with them. He knew without a shadow of a doubt that Emily couldn't have made those sounds, yet the voice coming through the playback sounded just like her, sobbing with fear and screaming *"Help me! Oh God - somebody please help me!"*

A heavy silence fell between them as they struggled with a terrible, rising fear. What was going on? What *could be* going on? They both fought down fears that they were out of their depth, floundering in the face of this new horror. Tyler shook himself to restore some normality to his wildly hammering heart and cleared his throat to get his voice back.

"I don't get it. First, we have someone walking around that looks like you. Now we have someone screaming for help that sounds like you. That's not just very, very weird. Hell - that's scary." Tyler continued, "What *is* going on here?"

"I'm not sure either, but this is totally freaking me out," Emily admitted, her chest still rising and falling visibly with the shock. Certainly, Tyler had never seen her look so white and drawn. Moving restlessly in her chair, she added tightly: "I'm not sure I can listen or watch much more of this right now. I think I'm going to go take a shower. Try to process this on my own for a bit. That's the real me, by the way, not my doppelganger." She forced herself to grin. Tyler decided to ignore her last comment.

"I totally get it. It's a bit... well... it's more than a bit...it's deeply unnerving," Tyler replied. He knew it was essential they try to maintain a business-like attitude instead of giving way to fear, or else they'd soon be jumping at their own shadows, so he said with a briskness he didn't really feel. "I'll keep going through the rest of the video since I'm about finished with the audio. Save me some hot water, though. Once we're dressed, we can head on into town. Maybe grab some dinner. Neither of us have eaten all day. And it will do us some good to be around other people - pretend we're normal, like them..." His lame attempt at humor fizzled out. She really wasn't in the mood. And neither, he had to admit, was he.

Emily got up and took the stairs to the master bedroom, hoping not to encounter any otherworldly spirits while she was in there. She immediately berated herself sternly "Girl, you need to pull yourself together! This is the kind of stuff you live for. This is why you do what you do." Though this time it was different. Finding evidence of the afterlife was great and all, but she didn't want it to *impersonate* her. That was a little too close for comfort and something she was not well versed on. Walking into the bathroom, she laid her clean clothes on the counter, and prepared herself for what she hoped would be the most relaxing hot shower of her life. Letting the room steam up a bit after turning on the hot water, she pulled the curtain back and stepped into the shower. The hot water ran down from the back of her head and down her body as she stood there with her eyes closed, facing the front of the shower. While her hands rubbed the soapy mixture through her hair, she heard rumbles of something falling and the faint click of the bathroom door - apparently opening. She peeked through the curtain but saw nothing. The door was closed, but there were a few bottles of travel shampoos and body wash lying under the shelves in the amenities closet where they hadn't been before.

Meanwhile, Tyler finished up the audio and video and began cutting clips of the evidence and placing them in their designated folders. He created links to the files on his new Word documents so the evidence could be kept together with each case file and easily accessible. Once completed, he stood up and stretched. The dining room chairs were not the most comfortable to sit in for long periods of time, and he had been perched there for almost three and a half hours. Parts of him were completely numb.

It was almost five and the sun had nearly set. Hunger had also set in, so he went to the pantry and opened the double doors, but failed to find anything that seemed appealing. He opened the refrigerator only to find the covered tray of leftovers from the first night. Even though they were Emily's, he didn't think she would mind and pulled back the foil cover.

'Yuuuckkk! Jeez!' He leaped back, his whole body quivering with revulsion. What had been a few french fries and a couple of chicken tenders were now a writhing mass of flies and maggots - hundreds of them crawling over everything. The stench was something else - long,

long dead and decomposing flesh. Hand over his nose and trying not to gag, Tyler quickly covered the tray, fumbling in his haste and disgust. Keeping the filthy thing at arms' length, he scrambled down the hall and out the front door, hoping that none of the little bastards fell out onto the floor. As soon as he got outside, he tossed the tray into the garbage can that sat close to the porch.

"Good riddance! You slimy bastards!" Tyler yelped, wiping his hands fiercely on his clothes and swallowing back vomit. He was still shaking with shock and visceral revulsion. Just as he got his act together enough to reenter the house, there stood Emily at the bottom of the stairs. Or did she?

"Is that really you?" he managed, through dry lips. Anything could happen now. Anything. This house was capable of anything.

"Yes, it's me. Fair enough question though," Emily shot back brusquely. "What just happened? Why all the hell-for-leather sprinting around?"

Suddenly Tyler felt very tired - no doubt the adrenaline seeping away. But he made a stab at a wry comment: "I hope you didn't want your leftovers."

"Ty, did you eat them?" Emily snarked, walking to the kitchen to check the refrigerator.

"Me? No. A Biblical plague of flies and maggots, yes!" Tyler snapped back at her while running up the stairs. "Now I'm getting in the shower so we can get the hell out of this house for a bit."

Emily yelled over the sounds of Tyler's heavy feet pounding on the steps: "Wait! How did maggots get onto my food from Monday night?"

"How the hell should I know?" Tyler hit back, "Check the seal of the door, maybe? I'll be back down in a minute."

Emily stood in the hallway, disgusted at the mere thought of maggots. She understood Tyler's frustration and revulsion. Upon his request, she investigated the refrigerator door - the seal was intact. It shouldn't have gotten warm inside - certainly not ridiculously so - as there had not been any power outages. Well, except for the DVR box. Then she realized that Tyler had gone upstairs to shower and hadn't taken any clothes. His return journey was going to be interesting. To avoid any uncomfortable situations, she grabbed her phone and decided to wait outside on the porch, watching the sun set. As she was sitting down in one of the rockers, an old 1970s-looking beat-up truck came pulled into the driveway.

"What the hell?" Emily said out loud to herself. Visitors were not on the agenda, and this was private property. Her only thought was that it could be the owners, yet surely, they would have called. She quickly looked down at her phone to see if there were any missed calls. Nothing. As the old pickup came to a stop, the gun rack lining the back window shook, and the driver side door opened. An older man stepped out of the vehicle. He was freakishly tall - maybe even 6' 6" - with broad shoulders and muscular build. Old he might be, but he was clearly not a weakling. Emily walked to the edge of the veranda.

"Howdy, Ma'am," the man said as he approached the walkway.

"Hi. Can I help you?" she said, a hint of concern in her voice.

"The name's Jeb. I live on the otha side of the pasture," the man said, pointing off in the distance.

Jeb didn't look like someone in their late 60s, though at times Emily - observant as she was - glimpsed hints of pain in his face. Presumably, farming had kept his body in shape, and he certainly looked like someone who could handle their own. His light brown hair was greased over the developing bald spot on the back of his head, while his eyes were barely visible under sagging eyelids. His mouth was covered by a neatly trimmed mustache.

Emily's secret obsession with serial killers kicked in and she immediately saw a striking resemblance to New Mexico's infamous David Parker Ray. Neighbor or not, she wasn't taking any chances. She remained silent, edging closer to the front door as the hairs on her arms and neck began to rise. Jeb continued to inch closer and closer to the porch, each footstep from his long muscular legs thudding slightly on the ground.

He quickly noticed her defensive body language and took a step back: "I'm sorry to have startled ya, miss. Ya see there, I just was wantin' to stop by and see who my new neighbors might be. Been seein' an awful lot of comin' and goin's past couple days. You out here alone?"

"I'm sorry. We're not neighbors. This is a rental. My husband and I are here for the week." She'd just lied, but Tyler wouldn't mind. Their strictly platonic relationship had its advantages. She'd hoped the mention of a "husband" might scare the guy away. Trying to remain calm, but by now her hand was on the doorknob, she continued: "I'm going to have to ask you to leave."

He let out a chuckle at the fear encompassing her every move and Emily could tell he found the whole scenario amusing: "Oh okay. Well, uh, I don't want no troubles. I guess I'll head on back to my truck then. No need to go gettin' all upset now. We don't want that now, do we?" Walking backward now down the walkway, he continued, "Just in case yer interested, I also wanted to tell ya, there's a Bible study, uh, going on tonight. Down yonder at the church if ya wanna come. It's down in the basement. We'd be mighty glad to have ya."

Bible studies were the last thing she wanted to hear about after the day she'd had. The thought turned her fear to anger. She couldn't stand anyone who pushed their religion onto others. Gripping the doorknob, she said forcibly: "No Thanks... Now, can you please leave?"

Continuing to chuckle under his breath, "Imma uh goin', but if ya head out anytime here soon, stop on by," Jeb said, finally turning his back and returning to the truck. He opened the driver's door, then touched one of the shotguns - hanging on the rack behind the seat - she hoped not meaningfully, and looked back. Emily was staring him down... *go, go, now!* He opened his mouth to say something else, but Emily quickly pointed towards the end of the driveway. Jeb got in and backed his battered old truck out of the property. The farther it got from the house the more relaxed Emily could feel herself becoming. Another unsettling incident in its way... At this point she was ready to call the whole investigation off and go home, but she couldn't do that to Tyler. Even yet, she couldn't run from her own fears.

Tyler came down the stairs from the shower wrapped in a towel. He skidded into the bedroom to get his clothes. As he quickly closed the door and turned to grab his suitcase, something caught his eye through the big windows - an old pickup backing down the driveway. Tyler hollered out for Emily, but she failed to respond. He grabbed some clothes and dressed himself as fast as he could. He yelled out again, before walking into the lobby. The front door was open. He started to peer around it when he collided - *smack!* - full-on with Emily just as she stepped back in. He got her right on the face.

"*Ouch!*" Tyler yelped.

"Ouch right back at you! I didn't know you were standing there," Emily said, stepping to the side of the door and rubbing her forehead.

"Not your fault. I was just peering out the door to see..." Tyler replied, "anyways, why didn't you answer me? I called a couple of times. And who was in that truck?"

"Let's not even talk about that. Some creepy old man trying to get us to go to a Bible study," she replied.

"You're kidding me!" Tyler remarked, rolling his eyes. But then his flippant mood was gone in an instant - suddenly he felt as if the whole place was closing in on him.

He wrapped his arms around his body, adding urgently: "We've gotta get out of here. I need food. And a drink!"

"Well, amen to that!" Emily smiled, adding mischievously, "Oh, and I might have told him you were my husband." They exchanged amused glances. As if!

"Hey, whatever you've gotta do to get rid of 'em." Tyler chuckled, exiting the house. He felt quite honored she deemed him fit enough for a husband, though it would never be possible. First off, her A-type personality would be cause for a divorce minutes into the marriage. Second off, girls were not his cup of tea.

By now it was almost seven and nightfall had settled all around like a dark velvet glove. Tyler decided to drive, mainly so that he could have control over the music they listened to. They were both heading for the car when Emily rushed back towards the house, explaining over her shoulder, "I forgot to leave a light on." With an amazing turn of speed, she sprinted into the house, turned on the porch light - it would be so much better to return to some friendly illumination - and nearly jumped back down the brick stairs, flinging herself breathlessly into the passenger seat.

"Scared much?" Tyler murmured, teasingly.

"Yes. It's creepy out here." Emily admitted, breathing hard.

Tyler plugged his phone into the car and started searching for some music to play. Not feeling like wasting too much time on it, he decided on a random Tori Amos playlist. Tori Amos soothed his soul. The way her fingers moved across the keys of a piano and the sounds she coaxed from it brought a deep peace to him. The lyrics of the songs took him to a whole new depth of emotion than any brainless pop music. After the day he had, he didn't care whether Emily wanted to listen to it or not. He needed it. He made a three-point turn in the driveway so that he didn't have to back all the way down - it would be asking for trouble to try to back out into that horrendous bend.

Emily sat in the passenger seat in deep thought while Tyler continued to sing his heart out. "Whatever makes him happy," she thought to herself and proceeded to gaze out the window. Her mind wandered onto the weird goings on in the house. What were they all about? Was it the land? Was it the accidents? Was it somehow the house itself? She didn't have the answers but hoped she could find them out. She closed her eyes and hoped they would come to her. When she reopened them, she felt a little frisson of excitement - and hope…

Emily saw a road sign in the front yard of another rundown farmhouse a short distance from where they were staying. The sign read:

Psychic Readings

Get all the answers to your questions here.

She hadn't noticed the sign before. There was a phone number at the bottom, but by the time she had read the top, they had already passed the sign and were steadily heading towards town. "Maybe it wouldn't be so bad to visit a psychic," Emily thought to herself. She had never used psychics during an investigation, but they did it on TV all the time. She would need to discuss it with Tyler and see how he felt about it. This would make for an interesting dinner conversation.

"Where are we going, anyways?" Emily asked, adjusting her position in the passenger seat.

Tyler abruptly stopped singing and stated sternly, "Food!".

"That's gonna be a plus," Emily replied, "But I was just wondering where we were going to actually get some."

"Oh, that I haven't thought of. I figured we would find something once we hit town," Tyler said.

"Let me check my phone and see if I can find anything appealing," Emily said, raising herself up to pull her phone out of her back pocket.

But opening the internet browser, instead of typing in places to eat, she found herself typing in "Psychics in Statesville, NC." So many names - she was surprised that there were so many options. The sign had not given a name, so she didn't know which one they had driven past. She clicked on the images tab at the top of the browser to check if maybe there was a picture of the sign she had seen, but there was nothing.

"Did you find anything?" Tyler asked.

"Oh, sorry. I got sidetracked there for a moment," Emily said, opening another browser and typing in "food near me."

"So, there's quite a lot to choose from," she said.

"I don't really care what we eat, as long as it's not crawling with…well you know." Tyler made a face like he was about to vomit all over the car.

"Hey, how about Applebee's?" Emily suggested. "There's always a good variety there, and it's close to Walmart. We can see if they have a DVR system there since this town has never heard of a Best Buy."

"Sounds good to me. We're not that far away either. I think I remember seeing it somewhere up here yesterday," Tyler said.

A few miles later he made a left-hand turn into a shopping center. This mall was complex consisting of a long row of shops interspersed with restaurants, with others set between the walkways. It was like a small town, with its own blocks and roads. The massive parking lot looked like it was designed for a theme park, but ninety percent of the spaces were empty. The majority of those taken were for Walmart, at the far end of the complex. Tyler eventually located the area of the car park nearest their destination. Stomach rumbling loudly, he hoped the food would be good, but the signs weren't looking great - there were no patrons outside or, it transpired, even inside the restaurant. The thought crossed his mind: "Why does everything in this town appear so ghostly?" It was as if the creepiness from the house was following them everywhere. Tyler shivered.

Night Three

Wednesday October 27, 2021

Tyler and Emily entered the restaurant through the double wooden doors and waited patiently at the host stand. They watched the employees loiter around the bar, talking instead of doing their jobs. Tyler began to get frustrated as hunger pains were nipping at his stomach, and yet again, it let out a loud rumble. Emily heard and realized food was getting urgent, waving down an employee airily sauntering past.

"Excuse me. Is there any way we could get seated?" Emily asked.

"Sure, just one second," the employee said, whizzing

past the host stand and making his way to the dim recesses of the restaurant.

Emily watched him whisper something into a young waitress' ear who giddily turned her head towards them. She couldn't have been more than sixteen and this was probably her first job. With that in mind, Emily tried to give them the benefit of the doubt. However, Tyler, as hungry as he was, probably wouldn't be so generous toward her. Emily let her A-type personality take control.

"How many?" the host asked, coming towards the stand.

"Two, please," Emily replied, with just that telling bit of snippiness in her voice.

"Right this way," the host murmured while she led the way to the table, carrying menus and wrapped silverware. She placed them down at a booth table in the far corner of the restaurant then looked up at Emily and Tyler as if daring them to ask for anything. Obviously from every last bit of body language and attitude, she thought they were complete pests. How dare they want food in a restaurant?

"Thank you," Emily said, with ironic emphasis, sitting down in the booth.

"Finally! God, I'm hungry!" Tyler exclaimed. He opened the menu… would it have chicken tenders and fries?

Five minutes later a waiter appeared at the table to take their orders. They decided to order everything at once, so that they didn't have to keep waiting for the server to return. To get things started off right, Tyler ordered a strawberry flavored Long Island iced tea, - just one, he reckoned. But then he really hadn't reckoned on drinking the giddy cocktail of vodka, tequila, light rum, triple sec and gin - and that excuse for a splash of cola - on a nearly empty stomach… He did also order an appetizer of cheese sticks to snack on before eating his meal of a blackened chicken alfredo, but it wasn't going to do much to offset the effect of the iced tea. At the moment, though, he didn't care. He just wanted relief from the tension of the endless weird stuff at the house. Emily ordered a rum and coke and a grilled chicken salad. The waiter walked off and stopped for a chat before heading to the kiosk to enter their orders. The wait had officially begun and they both placed bets on how long it would take for their food to arrive at the table. Neither won. Thirty-five-minutes later their wait was finally over, and the hunger pains could be put to ease.

"Man, it feels good to be out of that house now that we have food," Tyler said, leaning back contentedly. "I was half tempted to get in the car and go back to Winston Salem earlier."

"I had that thought too," Emily replied, before taking a bite of her salad. "But I talked myself out of it."

"Me too. I feel like we are on the brink of a great discovery," Tyler said. "We must be touching some kind of nerve, because things keep messing with our equipment."

"So, there's something I want to talk to you about. How do you feel about psychics?" Emily asked.

"I don't have anything against them. I don't know any personally," Tyler replied.

"I've never used psychics in an investigation before, but I think it could help give us some information that

Miss Sharon at the library can't provide," Emily continued, "We passed a place on the way here just down the road from the house. I think we should stop by tomorrow and see if he or she is willing at least to come do a walkthrough."

"You know, that's not a bad idea," Tyler agreed. "I bet that, since they're local, they know more about it than we'd be likely to find in a newspaper."

"That's what I was thinking. I'm glad you are on board, because I wasn't sure how well you'd respond to this idea," Emily said, welcoming her refilled rum and coke by drinking almost half of it immediately. Obviously, she is in a similar mood to Tyler - surrendering to a tiny bit of escape from the stress of the investigation.

Tyler grinned hugely when his second Long Island iced tea arrived, and then, continued to devour the pasta and the few grilled chicken strips he had left to eat - after all, there was no way he was taking leftovers back into that house. The two continued to bounce ideas off each other about plans for the continued investigation, which all seemed to center on whether the psychic would be willing to do a walkthrough. If it went well, they might even invite the psychic to investigate the house and grounds with them - and, come to think of it, on Halloween!

Once the tabs were settled, they headed towards the car, traveling the short distance into the Walmart parking area. Finding a parking space was easy enough since most of them still remained empty. They entered the store and walked to the back, where they hoped to find the electronics department.

"How did these kids even get here?" Emily commented, navigating through a dense group of teens who were blocking the main aisle.

"I don't know. Most of them don't appear old enough to drive. It's like their parents just dropped them off here and left. What time is it, anyways?" Tyler answered, looking down at his watch: it was almost a quarter after ten pm. "Don't they have school in the morning?"

When they walked into the spacious electronics area, they split up to search for anything related to a DVR system. Emily was the first to locate an aisle with options for a whole new system, but no individual DVR box. Tyler was unable to find anything helpful in the least - though he did find that he was getting increasingly lightheaded. The innocent-sounding iced tea was claiming yet another victim! He struggled to stand upright and slowly - but over firmly - walked over to Emily, where she was checking her money situation on her phone to see if she could just afford a whole new system.

"Heeeeyyyy. Did you find anythiinngg?" Tyler managed as he approached. Surely, he couldn't actually be slurring, could he?

"I did. You good though?" Emily asked, peering at him critically.

"I might be a little buzzed. I think thosh teas - two laaarrrrgggeee teas, ha! - were a lot sssshtronger than I was expecting. Definitely shhhneaks up on ya," Tyler slurred, swaying back and forth, body showing a distinct tendency to bounce off the store's shelves. "Oooopsh…' He burped, repressing a giggle.

"You're a lightweight. Give me the keys," Emily said, as sternly as she could while trying not to smile -

though as quickly as she had drunk her rum and Cokes, she was surprised she didn't have much of a buzz. They must not have been very strong.

"Yeeaaaahhhhh, you might wanna drive back," Tyler admitted, slowly plopping the keys into her hand. "I think… I think… Imma wade my way through those teenage Walmart groupies… head over to the grosshhery area and find a snack. That might…*Hic*…" Tyler choked on his words as he let out the loudest hiccup that resonated throughout the electronics department. He chuckled at the sound then continued: "might help me…shhhober up a bits"

Emily, holding in a painful laugh, watched as Tyler lurched down the main aisle towards the food - the sounds of his hiccups fading into the distance. When he was out of sight, she let out the laughter she couldn't hold in any longer. Finally, wiping away a tear - which she was glad Tyler hadn't seen - resuming her quest to obtain the surveillance equipment, she spotted a lonely cart sitting in an aisle. She grabbed it and made her way back to the electronics department. Picking the cheapest system available, she hurled it over into the cart. Now, she needed to find out where Tyler had wandered off to.

Tyler was meandering unsteadily around the Little Debbie cakes on the snack aisles when Emily pulled up with the cart. He noticed the surveillance system box and figured she had made the decision to replace the whole thing. Reunited - he grabbed a box of pinwheels off the shelf - they headed up to the checkout, paid and walked back out to the car. Emily got in the driver's seat and had to adjust it forward to reach the gas and brakes. Tyler wasn't that tall so all that adjusting made her feel really short. Meanwhile, he just lay back in his passenger seat and passed out immediately.

Emily drove slowly, mainly because it wasn't her car, but she also wanted to get a better look at the sign advertising the psychic. As she approached the house she slowed down even more. There was no traffic around, so she saw no problem slowing down long enough to snap a picture of the sign with her phone. The only problem was that it was almost completely dark. There were no signs of light anywhere and Emily feared she may have passed the psychic's house already. Suddenly, out of nowhere came a large cargo truck plowing towards her. The headlights were much brighter due to the immense darkness and nearly blinded her as she brought the car to a complete stop in the middle of the road.

After the truck had passed and the afterimage of the lights faded from her retinas, she caught the slightest reflection of light on the sign. How convenient that the truck happened to be passing just as she was passing the house. Even more convenient that it brought her to a complete stop right in front of it. Since it was dark and there were no lights on inside the old farmhouse, she slowly pulled into the driveway. She turned the headlights off and exited the car but left it running in case she needed to make a quick escape. Emily walked over to the sign in the front yard. She pulled her phone out of her back pants pocket, turned on her flash and took a picture of the sign. She now had a phone number and would call it first thing in the morning to set up an appointment. Returning to the car, she quietly closed the door. Tyler had slept through the whole thing, but she'd tell him in the morning. Maybe.

Emily drove the short distance back to the house. When she pulled into the drive, the first thing she noticed was that the porch light was no longer on and, it seemed, neither were the inside lights. She pulled up in the driveway, and reached over to poke Tyler's shoulder, maybe none-too gently.

"Tyler. Come on. Wake up. We're back and, um, there are no lights on."

Tyler stirred in the passenger seat then hauled himself to a rough approximation of a sitting position. After blinking hard a few times, he managed to pull the lever to raise the seat upright. He looked around in a bit of a daze. There was nothing but darkness - briefly letting fear start to set in - he felt the hairs on the back of his neck begin to rise. But that wasn't useful. He shook himself - come on Tyler, get moving! Don't let the side down! (By which he realized he meant don't piss Emily off again.) He soon remembered he'd put a small flashlight in the glove box a couple weeks before and immediately tried to locate it. In the dark he felt his hands touching everything but what he was looking for. Suddenly, his shaking hands touched a round metal cylinder with a rubbery button on it. He had found it. Pushing the rubber button on the end, the car was engulfed with light.

"Hey! Hey! You good? It's okay," Emily said, trying to calm him down. "But I'm glad you have this flashlight tucked away in here. I wasn't looking forward to going back inside in the dark."

"Yeah, yeah. I'm good," Tyler answered, trying to catch his breath from the fear. "Sorry, I tripped out for a moment there. But, seriously, what the hell? Why are the lights out?"

"I don't know, but I'm sure as hell going to find out," Emily said, opening the car door and walking around to the passenger door to open it for Tyler.

"Thanks." Tyler said, struggling up from his seat and shining the light up toward the house.

"I'm not going anywhere without you. You have the light," Emily pointed out.

"True. Let's get inside. The sound of the trees rustling in the breeze is creeping me out." Tyler made a beeline - or what in his current state passed for a beeline

- for the steps up to the porch. Emily followed closely behind and then realized she was the one with the key to the house. Walking up on the porch, Tyler shined the flashlight around to check for anything that might be out of place. Seeing that everything appeared to be fine, he moved the light onto the door. Emily slid the key into the keyhole, but before she could unlock it, the door suddenly swung open slightly, as if slyly inviting them to come inside. Just as it had on the first night they had arrived. They both looked at each other, a hint of fear in their eyes, but still proceeded inside the house.

The two of them slowly entered the house, not sure what to expect on the other side of the door. To their surprise everything appeared to be as they had left it - other than the light switches had been turned off.

"I don't believe it!" Tyler exclaimed, rushing from room to room turning on every light he could find. "How did the lights turn out?"

"I'm just as confused as you are. Maybe the power went out?" Emily looked at the time and it was nearly close to midnight.

"There could be a short in the electrics, or maybe they're on some kind of timer." Tyler started to check electrical outlets and walls for any type of device that would back up his theory. "We should contact the owners. They would know if there was a timer on or not."

"It's after midnight. We can't call them now..."

Tyler looked at her, shaking his head, strongly insisting they be the first ones they called in the morning. If it were up to him, he would have already called them when the maggots appeared in the fridge.

This latest little bit of strangeness justified Emily's decision to stay downstairs and sleep on the couch again. She didn't trust being alone upstairs. Tyler went into his room. He was still a bit tipsy, although the sudden excitement of waking up in the dark had sobered him a little. As he closed the door to prepare himself for hopefully the best night of sleep in his life, he started to laugh at how they depended on a flashlight when they could have just used the ones on their phones, doubling the amount of available light. He stumbled over to the bed and pulled the sheets back - not even noticing that the bed had been made up again. He dropped heavily onto the mattress and, forgetting to pull the covers over him, passed out again.

The house remained silent for the first few hours of sleep. It wasn't until around three in the morning that it started to come alive - impossibly but really… Emily was jolted from a deep sleep by the sound of what appeared to be lively chattering in the kitchen. She flung the comforter over the back of the couch and stumbled over to the light switch, before creeping shakily down the hallway still half asleep. She was grateful that the light came on obediently when she pressed the switch. As she neared the kitchen, she turned the light on and peeked around the door. No one. Standing in sheer silence, she listened - but soon discovered that the voices had faded from the kitchen and were now coming from the very room where she'd been sleeping.

Emily turned into the dining room and picked up

one of the audio recorders left there from their evidence review the previous day. Turning it on, she carried it with her, edging closer back into the living room. The voices appeared to be resonating from the wall between the two rooms. She pressed her ear to the wall and listened intently to make out anything that was being said - but no, sadly, still nothing was intelligible. She sat the recorder on the coffee table and lay back down on the couch for what seemed like hours trying to make out the words coming from the walls around her. Wondering if Tyler could hear them, she got up and walked over to peek into his room. He was snoring loudly and showed no signs of being disturbed by anything. She quietly closed the door so that she wouldn't wake him and went into the kitchen to make some coffee. By now seriously sleep deprived, she was aching with tiredness. It was going to take some seriously strong caffeine to keep her going right now, let alone over the next few days.

Sitting at the kitchen island she heard a screen door slam closed - and suddenly the voices came to a halt. This was rather odd as the house didn't actually have a screen door. Emily got up and began walking from room to room to check if there was anything that would account for that sound. By the time she'd made it upstairs, the sun had started to rise on the horizon, and she could see the glimmers of daylight through all the windows. Under any other circumstances, she would have reveled in this glorious light - but now there was just relief that the darkness had lifted. But even so, the house was still a brooding menace.

A few seconds later she found herself standing in the library staring at all the books that lined the walls. "There's got to be more relevant information somewhere in all those," she thought, and began opening each of the cabinets one by one, sifting through the titles on each spine.

When she reached her fourth bookcase, she happened across *The Nichol's Family: A Tragic Ending*. Aha! Maybe this was what she'd been looking for. Tiredness lifting, she flipped through the pages. It was filled with old pictures of the house and various members of the family dating back to the mid 1800's. She checked to see when the book had been published: 1955. Just three years after Mary Nichols' death. Emily sat down, determined to make the most of the book. Looking through the table of contents, she found a chapter devoted to Mary and William, which confirmed that they had indeed been the owners of the property she was currently sitting in. As she continued to read, she came across a family name that she had not heard before: Sullivan. According to the book, the Nichols and the Sullivan families had both settled into the area just a few years apart. The Sullivans had a history of running new settlers off in order to lay claim to the properties surrounding theirs - building their empire. When the Nichols family arrived, the Sullivans felt that the property should belong to them because they got there first, though they had no legal claim to it.

This started a century-long feud between the two families. Over time the Sullivans began to lose their control over the area and their fortune dwindled away after the stock market crash of 1929. They were forced to sell off parcels of land just to survive. Due to the lack of finances flowing in from the vast amounts of farmlands they had once acquired, the Sullivans had to look for other ways to bring in money - though they never gave up the dream of one day - taking over the Nichols property. The Nichols remained on the land until the death of Mary in 1952 when the house was willed to their housekeeper and caretaker Lilith Sullivan, a young single mother with one child.

Emily was so engrossed in the book that she had forgotten she had started making coffee down in the kitchen. Its inviting, fresh aroma reaching her, she jumped up, taking the book with her. When she rounded the bottom of the stairs, she noticed the door to Tyler's room was now open, and that he was no longer passed out on the bed. She grabbed the recorder she had placed on the stairs, pressed the stop button, and walked into the kitchen to find a surprisingly on-the-ball Tyler pouring himself a cup of coffee. She must have been so focused on the book that she hadn't even heard him walking around downstairs. She was glad that he was up.

It would mean that they could get an early start on setting up their new surveillance system. It also meant they could make the necessary phone calls to find out why the lights were turned off while they were out. Emily was even more thrilled that it meant they could reach out to the psychic and try to schedule a walkthrough for the house. Her to-do list was adding up: today was going to be an eventful day.

Day Four

Thursday October 28, 2021

"Good morning," Emily said as she walked into the kitchen and picked up a clean coffee cup from the counter. "How did you sleep?"

"Good morning. I slept pretty well. How about you?" Tyler replied. He was certainly more bright-eyed and alert this morning.

"Eh, not so much. Been up for the last couple hours. The voices were here again last night," Emily responded, holding up the audio recorder and explaining her experiences of just a few hours before.

"That's interesting. I can start reviewing that once

I've had some coffee and maybe a couple Tylenol," Tyler replied. Maybe he wasn't so on the ball after all.

"Oh, of course." Emily held up the unusable DVR. "I'd really like to get this thing replaced and up and running before we start any evidence review. I don't want a single inch of this house unrecorded."

"Have you called the owners yet?" Tyler asked.

"No. I was waiting for you to wake up. Let me do that now," Emily got up from the bar stool and went into the living room to retrieve her phone.

When she came back, she had her phone on speaker so that she and Tyler could both communicate with the owners. The phone rang and rang but there was no answer - and it eventually went to a voicemail.

"The party you are trying to reach is not available and the voicemail box is full. Please try your call again later. Thank you." The recording played.

Emily hung up and opened the Airbnb application - hopefully she could reach them through the app. At least she would be able to leave them a message asking them to call her. She typed it into the "Contact Your

Host" option and tapped send.

"Well, that's the only thing I know to do at the moment," she remarked, looking at Tyler. "I'll keep my phone close by just in case they call back."

"That's all we can do, I guess, except pack up and leave this place," Tyler nodded, but deep down he didn't want to do that. He enjoyed the thrill of the investigation, but right now he just wanted answers to the weird stuff that had happened. He took his last sip of coffee before heading out to retrieve the surveillance equipment from the car.

"Hey, where did you leave the car keys last night?" he asked Emily.

"They should be in the living room on the coffee table."

Tyler walked towards the living room, looking up the stairs as he passed. He had a strong sense that someone was watching him, though that was a constant feeling in this house. He found the car keys lying on the coffee table, just as Emily had said, and walked out to the car. He grabbed the box of new equipment from the trunk and carried it inside, figuring that as he was responsible for all tech, it would be up to him to reset everything. That was ok. It was what he wanted after all.

Emily sat at the kitchen counter unplugging all the cords from the old DVR, as Tyler was opening the new box and pulling out the contents. She was hopeful that all they would have to do was switch them out from one box to the other. Tyler passed her the new DVR and, thankfully, it had the same connecting ports as the previous one. It also came with four additional ones, so they could add four more cameras throughout the house. Once the existing cameras were connected, they started deciding where to position the new four. They both agreed that one or two should go on the porch to record any outside occurrences. It would also keep record of any unexpected visitors. They decided to put an additional one in the hallway, shooting up the stairway. The remaining one they placed in the upstairs hallway facing Emily's room. If anything walked in, they were going to catch it.

As Emily sat at the counter testing the video feeds from each camera, she explained to Tyler the information she had found in the book. Tyler listened intently while he was hooking up the audio recorder to his computer in the dining room. There was a brief moment where he felt some sympathy for the Sullivans, who went from being a predominant local family in the area to having nearly nothing. With that sympathy came a feeling of concern, wondering how the one thing the Sullivans had sought after, they finally ended up getting in the end.

"Does it say why the house and land was left to her?" Tyler asked. "Wasn't there any other relative it could have gone to?"

"I didn't really get much farther," Emily responded. "I'll have to plow on once I have a chance. I feel like this book is going to have quite a bit of information. It's already given us the name of the old lady who is said to be haunting the place. We can use this tonight in our next investigation."

"I wonder if there is some way to view a copy of the will?" Tyler asked. "Do they keep things like that on public record?"

"Let me Google it," Emily replied. "I'm honestly not sure."

Emily typed the question of whether wills are made public record after a person passes away into Google on her phone and awaited a response. Almost immediately, the results popped up: apparently in North Carolina wills will not become public until the creator has passed and the executor files it with the clerk of court. So. there *was* a chance they could view the will, which might shed some light as to why the house was left to Lilith in the first place.

"Looks like we will be paying another visit to Sharon," Tyler commented, pulling a face.

"Yep. God, I hope she's in a better mood than last time," Emily said. "They should be open today - at least that's what she said before."

"Sounds good. I'll go through this audio from last night and hop in the shower afterwards," Tyler nodded. "Are we stopping by the psychic's place as well?"

Emily stared, then remembered she hadn't told him about getting the phone number on the way home the night before.

"I managed to grab the telephone number from the

sign last night while you were passed out," she pointed out, keeping it simple.

"Oh, ok, cool," he replied.

"Yeah, I'll give them a call in just a moment, while you work on that," Emily said.

Tyler nodded, securing his earphones tightly over his ears. He started the audio playback. Once Emily had all the surveillance equipment and cameras ready to record, she started the DVR recording and once again the house was fully monitored. Good! She picked up her phone to find the photo of the psychic's sign. Dialing the number, she waited nervously, not knowing what to expect when - or if - someone answered the phone.

"Hello. Lorelai's Readings. What future can I share with you today?" the sing-song voice down the line intoned. It was obvious she'd said this line hundreds of times and was more than slightly bored.

"Hi. My name's Emily Adair," Emily introduced herself. "I'm the leader of the Winston-Salem Paranormal Research Group, and we are here in Statesville conducting an investigation on the Nichols property. We were wondering if you have done or would be interested in doing a walkthrough of it for us, and, if so, how much would you charge?"

"Well, my name is Lorelai, and by walkthrough, you mean give a reading of the land and house? I try not to go into that area very often. The energies there get the best of me at times." She wasn't the only one, Emily thought wryly.

"Ah, I see. Well, that's too bad. We were hoping that someone local would be able to help us validate some of our findings this week," Emily said. "Is there any way you would be willing to meet with us outside of the property?"

"Well, yes. I could do that," Lorelai responded. "How about tomorrow? Let's see. Let me check my appointment calendar."

"We greatly appreciate this," Emily said, thankful that she would at least get to sit and discuss some of the weirder events that increasingly preoccupied her. She hoped that by meeting with the psychic she might convince her to come and investigate with them.

"Yes, I think I can make tomorrow work. Though it will have to be later on in the evening. How about around seven?" Lorelai suggested. "Since it's so late, I'll make us all dinner and we can sit around the table and have a chat."

"Oh, thank you," Emily replied, taken aback but delighted. "You don't have to make dinner, though."

"I insist!" Lorelai responded firmly. "We'll see you then."

Lorelai immediately hung up. No goodbyes, no nothing. Emily didn't care. She was excited to even get to the psychic, who apparently kept a very busy schedule. Leaving her phone in the kitchen, she went into the dining room where she softly tapped Tyler on the shoulder and was interested to see that he jumped at the unexpected touch. They were both getting jumpy - and with good reason. Just how good they'd no doubt discover from Lorelei's visit.

"Hey, we're having dinner tomorrow night with the psychic," Emily told him rather pleased with herself.

"Dinner? Do we know her that well? Should we be

eating these people's food?" Tyler questioned, suddenly snippy.

"Ouch! That's a bit of an extreme reaction, don't ya think?"

Tyler removed his earphones, and turning in the chair, continued: "I just don't know how I feel about this. I thought we were going to get her to come here." Their experiences with people in this town hadn't been the greatest, and he didn't feel like entering an unknown person's home in the middle of nowhere. Extreme reaction? Maybe, but on the hand, he felt it was totally justified.

"I tried," Emily replied. "But she wouldn't do that, and this is the only way we could get to see her. She's the one that literally insisted on dinner."

"Probably so that she can poison us with some kind of potion," Tyler murmured, trying to sound flippant, but alarming himself by wondering if part of him actually meant it.

"She's a psychic, not an alchemist, silly. Now you're just being paranoid," Emily soothed - sometimes, he thought, she could be insufferably condescending - even patting him on the shoulder. "I'm going to go upstairs and get ready to head into town. How much do you have left to review?"

"About another forty-five minutes or so," Tyler replied. "I should be done by the time you finish getting dressed and then I can jump in the shower."

Tyler went back to reviewing the audio file, while Emily turned to the stairs. As she walked by the staircase, the door to the cupboard underneath popped open. Kind of strange, she thought, as it hadn't done that beforehand. She chalked it up to possibly stepping on a floorboard that may have caused it to open. Closing it securely, she continued up the stairs.

Tyler's review of the audio file turned up nothing. There were sounds of what could have been voices from a distant location, but nothing intelligible. He did, however, hear what was obviously a screen door closing - as in a non-existent screen door - and then Emily getting up to investigate. He decided to cut this audio clip and store it in the house file since it had captured a sound that could not be explained. With a fresh cup of coffee in hand, he sat and watched the camera screens on the monitor. There was Emily, emerging from the bedroom - closing the door behind her - and started walking down the stairs. He got up and went to meet her at the bottom of the stairs, where he briefly explained his findings on the audio - then ran up the stairs to shower. With a fresh aromatic cup of coffee, she picked up her now essential reading and sat outside on one of the old rocking chairs while waiting for Tyler.

The morning air was distinctly brisk, but it felt good on her after being warmed up from the hot shower. She placed her coffee cup on one of the side tables and, opening the book where she had left off, continued to read. The book opened to a double page spread showing a breakdown of the Nichols family tree. While it appeared the tree ended with the childless William and Mary, there was another branch connected to Mary. It seemed she had a sister, Elizabeth - who was married to a Wilbur Jennings and the chart showed they had one son, Andrew. If this family tree was accurate, Emily wondered, why wasn't the property left to Elizabeth and her family when Mary died? What happened that caused her to leave the family home to their rivals? And who actually owned the property now? The people listed as the owners on Airbnb weren't called Sullivan so apparently the house had changed hands again at some point. Emily was left with more questions than answers - and not for the first time.

Having seen Emily out on the porch from his bedroom window, the newly showered and dressed Tyler went out to join her. As he emerged from the house, he noticed with some small satisfaction that it was her turn to jump.

"You startled me," she said, adding smugly: "You're never going to believe what I found out."

"Try me," Tyler replied.

"So, Andrew Jennings was related to the Nichols. The same Nichols that owned this house," Emily went on to explain the breakdown of the family tree and his relevance.

"No way! Well, yet more questions than answers,"

Tyler said. "I hope we can find out more from the actual will. Are you ready to head out?"

"Yeah, let me grab a few things and I'll be ready," Emily tidily took her cup back indoors.

She insisted on taking her car while grabbing a notebook and pen from the dining room table, along with the Nichols family book. Swinging his backpack over his shoulder Tyler asked:

"Should we leave any lights on?"

"We can at least try," Emily replied.

As they exited the house, she made doubly sure to leave the hall and porch lights on again. They securely closed the door behind them, turning the doorknob hard and pushing on the door twice to ensure that it was truly locked. Once in the car, Emily proceeded to back out of the driveway. Tyler was trying not to look resentful, but Emily had made it clear she wanted to drive. He didn't like going places where his car wasn't accessible in case he needed to make a quick escape. This ritual had started, when as a teenager, he'd been stranded at a party where he no longer wished to be. He still shuddered at the unbidden memories of the Party from Hell. Sometimes swift getaways were essential.

The drive to the library didn't seem to take as long as the last time, probably because they were more familiar with the area and were able to navigate around it a little better. It was close to noon by the time they arrived. Emily found a parking space close to the door and they both grabbed their stuff and headed off to brave Miss Sharon in her lair. There was no one at the counter when they entered - phew! - but just when they thought they were saved from having to deal with her again, here came the unmistakable shuffle of white Reebok Classics towards them.

"Well, well...Good morning," Sharon said, adding unnecessarily: "I see you have come back. What brings you in here this time? More ghouls and goblins?" She sat down at her computer, frowning ferociously.

"We're wondering if there's any way that we could view a will on public record," Emily explained.

"That's gonna depend on whether it has been digitized," Sharon snipped back. "If it's not on our computer, you're gonna need to go down to the courthouse and request a copy. Which is probably what you are going to have to do anyways."

"Can you please check?" Tyler asked, trying to sound polite, but still noticed a steely undertone creeping into his voice.

"No, but you can," Sharon quipped and pointed over to a row of computers along the back wall.

"OK," Emily acknowledged. "Can you at least tell us what site we need to be checking to get us the best results?"

"You could try the National Will Register's site," Sharon replied. "But you'll probably have to go to the courthouse to get a physical copy. I can almost guarantee it." She turned her attention to her screen, waving them away as if batting flies.

"Thanks," Emily said, smiling insincerely, as she and Tyler walked over to the computers. There were five along the back wall, but none were in use. Tyler and Emily picked the farthest two away from the front counter and decided that it would be best if they both did the search. Tyler wanted to find an obituary for Mary Nichols to see if any living relatives were mentioned, after all, that could confirm the information in the Nichols book. They both settled in, making notes along the way of which sites they had visited and what the search results turned up.

Emily's search of the National Will Register was proving to be difficult, though it did provide a list of all wills that had gone through probate after the death of the individual. Thankfully, Sharon had not been correct. Emily was able to search by the name and date of death, which she'd taken from the Nichols book. After several tries of entering the information in different formats, she succeeded in pulling up a digital copy of Mary's will. At last. But would it move their research much farther on? Still, just sitting there with it up on screen was promising - even rather exciting.

Tyler's search was much easier since Statesville documented just about everything in the papers. He found multiple sites that provided access to Mary's obituary, though the information in it was about as basic as they come. It listed a few short snippets about Mary's life and the date and times for the funeral service. There was no mention of any living relatives who could have verified the information in the book. Out of the corner of his eye, Tyler saw Emily walk over to the printer.

"That will be ten cents per page!" he heard Sharon yell from her desk. That woman had eyes like a hawk.

Emily nodded in acknowledgement and returned to the computer station. She flipped through the pages, but they were mostly in a bunch of legal jargon she didn't fully understand. It wasn't until she got to page six that she realized she was just getting to the good stuff. She tapped Tyler on the arm on which his chin was resting.

"Hey," she whispered. "I think I've found it."

"Really - wow!" he replied. "Let's see what it says."

"Hold on," Emily said. "Let me print another copy. That way you can have your own. I can barely read this up close, let alone at a distance."

Emily clicked "print" and headed over once more to the printer. Handing Tyler his copy, she told him to begin on page six. They both examined their documents, reading quietly until Emily came across something that really leaped out. All living relatives in the Nichols book were mentioned in Mary's will. This made Tyler wonder who'd written the obituary since it seemed to disregard a single living relative. They continued reading, until they came across the part that discussed the fate of Mary's assets.

The will stated that all assets would be set up into a trust that would go to her nephew, Andrew Jennings. Considering that Andrew was only 16 when Mary passed away, the will stated he would not be able to access the trust, which included the property and house, until he married. Tyler and Emily found this a bit odd, as normally most people received their inheritance when they turned 18 or became an adult. The age requirement for adulthood varied in different states and has changed over time. The will went on to say that until this marriage occurred, the house and property would continue to be looked after by the housekeeper and former caretaker of Mary Nichols, Lilith Sullivan, where she would be allowed to remain in residence with her one child - though their name was not mentioned. Lilith would continue to receive her monthly pay from the trust until Andrew was able to legally come into his property.

"So, according to this, Lilith Sullivan would have to give up the land that her family so desperately desired when Andrew got married," Tyler paraphrased.

"That's what it seems like," Emily agreed. "Except he never got married, because they all died in the car accident."

"In front of that house…" Tyler said.

"It makes sense as to why they were in the area," Emily added, nodding slowly, as much to herself as to Tyler. "Maybe he was taking Carol out there to show her what she would be getting once they were married."

"That's a possibility," Tyler said. "But the investigator in me has even more questions. It seems the more we find answers the more questions arise. Like, this woman's finances were about to get cut off. She was about to lose the place she had lived in for God knows how long. How do you not think that she had something to do with this accident? And then not to answer the door when Carol came running up for help? I just don't understand."

"Keep your voices down over there! This is a library!" Sharon yelled across the room, with no sense of irony. But it was true that Tyler's excitement had given his voice a certain insistence in the quiet of the room.

"Questions are good," Emily replied in a stage whisper. "But let's keep in mind we are paranormal investigators, not detectives or police officers."

"It's the same concept," Tyler argued. "We investigate to find evidence. We then take that evidence and compare it with documentation, should that need arise. If we can't find anything to back it up, then we must throw most of it out. We also spend a lot of time trying to debunk evidence. I just feel like there should have been more investigation of the accident. Especially after finding this out."

Emily sat there and let what Tyler had said sink in. She never really thought of comparing their sort of research with police officers' or the FBI.

While she was deep in thought, Tyler turned back to the computer and began searching for more information on the accident that occurred in October 1961. His frustration had now erased his residual sympathy for the Sullivans. This time he didn't want to know the cause of death. He wanted to know the outcome. What happened *after* these people died? Was there any type of investigation into Lilith and her family? Tyler scrolled through online article after article trying to find answers. Apparently - and incredibly - no investigation had taken place. It was just considered to be another tragic accident on a curve that had claimed many other lives over the years. He was about to give up on his search when the last article he was reading stated the name of the police chief who responded to the accident, Chief Seth Sullivan.

"Bingo!" Tyler nearly shouted. He looked back to the counter in anticipation of Sharon's next scolding, but she was no longer guarding her territory, dragon-like. "Look at this!"

"This doesn't prove anything, Tyler," Emily said, though acknowledging to herself it was quite interesting that the Sullivans - or at least *a* Sullivan - had been involved one way or another. “Maybe there’s another Sullivan family in the area? It’s a possibility. I’m just saying, consider all the possible factors here.”

“No, you’re right. It could be another family all together, but I bet he is the reason the case was quickly closed and just made to look like another accident,” Tyler objected, feeling increasingly impassioned.

“Unfortunately, we will never know,” Emily said.

“Well, this definitely gives us something more substantial for our investigation tonight,” Tyler said while clicking “print” on the computer screen. “I’m bringing this with us, that way we’ll have it for reference. We can add it to the accident file later.”

“Let’s do some research on the police chief,” Emily suggested. “That way we know what kind of person he was, before we just go assuming things.”

“I’m down for that,” Tyler replied. He quickly started another Google search on Police Chief Sullivan. It transpired he was a decorated serviceman. He had served aboard the *USS North Carolina* during World War II alongside many of his fellow classmates.

Becoming one of the injured during a Japanese torpedo attack that occurred on September 15, 1942, he received an honorable discharge from service. Returning to his home state, he decided to go into law enforcement, where he quickly made a name for himself by solving multiple past and current crimes. Some even dubbed him the "American Sherlock Holmes". In the mid-1950s he was promoted to police chief, remaining in that post until his retirement in 1977. During this time, he led what some would describe as a brutal police force, though crime in the area dropped twenty-five percent while he was in charge. His death occurred in 1985 from cancer. It seemed the only bad thing they could find on this man was the fact that he smoked and was quite the tyrant in his governing of law enforcement.

"See, I seriously doubt this man covered up some kind of foul play surrounding Andrew's accident," Emily pointed out, thinking hard, after they'd read all the articles Tyler had pulled up on the computer.

"I guess you're right," he replied. "Something still just doesn't seem right about it. I don't know. Maybe I am searching for something that's not there."

"I think you're right about that," Emily acknowledged. "How about we pack up and go grab a bite to eat before we head back to the house? No drinks this time! We have work to do this evening."

"Sounds good," Tyler answered. "I'm getting hungry. We forgot to eat lunch again."

They packed up their notes, keeping out the printed pages, and went to pay the printing fees.

"Oh, this is a lot. I'm gonna have to charge you ink fees as well," Sharon crowed triumphantly, checking her handy chart for how many pages constituted a one-dollar additional ink fee. "Well, I guess not this go round. You're just shy of the page count. That's gonna be two dollars and thirty cents."

Tyler pulled out his wallet and handed Sharon three dollars.

"Oh, no," Sharon said. Boy, was she loving this! "We don't give change. Oh, and you're not gonna make it to the courthouse in time. They closed around three today. I guess I should have told you that when you got here."

"Actually, we don't need to," Emily stepped briskly up to the counter, adding. "And keep the change. Add it to the ink fee fund - if need be." She added under her breath, "Go on, enjoy yourself…"

Tyler didn't care about the change and probably would have made the same decision, but even still, it wasn't Emily's to just be handing out freely. Yet again, another inconsiderate move on her part. She dragged him out the door before he could agree. She later explained that she would pay for dinner to make up for the change, but that she had to get away from that woman.

Once in the car, Tyler asked, "Why do you dislike that woman so much? I get it, she's a bit snippy and set in her ways, but is that really a reason to be rude to her?"

"Honestly, she reminds me of my mom," Emily replied. "She always has something negative and judgmental to say when it comes to researching the paranormal."

"That's understandable, but she's not your mom," he said. "She's just doing her job."

There was a brief moment of silence, then Tyler looked over at Emily and said, "You never talk about your mom. But I'm sorry there's tension between the two of you."

"It's ok." Emily paused, having a flashback of the happier times before her mother had left. She only remembered a few, but she cherished them. She wiped a tear away, trying not to show any sign of weakness. As group leader, there was no room for a softy, but as more memories flooded her mind, more tears started to flow. But it wasn't until Tyler reached over, placing his hand on her shoulder, that her iron control gave way.

This was a side of her Tyler had never seen before. She was the kind of person who kept her personal life to herself, and always maintained a tight control over her emotions. But Tyler didn't look at her as weak just because she had shed a tear. He saw someone who was truly hurting inside. Maybe it was the lack of sleep that had brought her to this breaking point.

"You know I'm here if you ever need to talk."

Wriggling uncomfortably, Emily pulled herself

together enough to mutter, "Thank you. I'll be ok."

"Do you mind if I ask what happened?" Tyler continued hesitantly, not wanting to trigger a complete breakdown, but deep down truly wanting to know the troubles of the girl sitting beside him.

"You know I don't talk about my mom often," she said. "I guess I don't handle the legitimacy of our work being questioned. It's something she does all the time. Something she has done since…" Emily seemed to be staring down a long tunnel into the past she'd rather not recall. Then briskly she said, "We probably should be on our way."

"We can sit here as long as you need. After all, you're the one with the keys," Tyler said, pulling a wry face to try to make her laugh.

Gratifyingly, Emily let out a short laugh - but then immediately reeled it back in. She continued to explain her situation as a teenager in the suffocating church environment. Afterwards, she explained, her mom refused to talk with her and continued to sermonize about how much she and her father were going to burn in hell because of their choices. But while Emily's father had stood by her during this time and respected her wishes, she knew her relationship with her mother would never be the same. And now seeing Sharon, who bore a strong resemblance to her mom - they dressed the same, acted the same, and to her, they were pretty much the same - brought it all back.

"Emily, I'm so sorry you had to experience all that," Tyler responded to her uncharacteristic emotion. "I need you to understand, though, she really isn't your mother."

"I know. I know. Sometimes it's just really hard for me to separate the two - between those that remind me of her and my actual mom. You'd be surprised how many snippy older women with bad hair and even worse dress sense there are around… Anyways, where are we eating tonight? Anywhere but Applebees," she said, answering herself before Tyler could speak.

"I'm ok with fast food," he replied. "We could pick up a pizza on the way back. Although I'm not crazy about bringing food back into the house…" he trailed off, the sight and stink of those mystery maggots looming large in his mind. Shaking himself to banish the memory he said in a business-like tone: "Speaking of, did the owners of the house ever get back in touch with you?"

"No, they haven't. I'm going to call them again right now," she said, picking up her phone and dialing the number.

"The party you are trying to reach is not available and the voicemail box is full. Please try your call again later. Thank you," the recording played.

"This is really strange," Tyler commented. "What about the Airbnb messenger?"

Emily opened the app, but unsurprisingly there was no response. "It doesn't look like they've even checked it."

Emily began to feel concerned for the situation and could tell Tyler felt the same. Maybe, this sort of silence was usual for the owners once their house was rented out. But although most hosts at least try to be available for their guests in case of emergencies, these people were impossible to contact. She didn't even have a home address for them, but assuming it was the same as the house, that wouldn't do them any good. But seeing as the owners weren't actually in the house, they must have another address.

"That's nuts." Tyler shook his head disbelievingly.

"Agreed. I'll keep trying throughout the night," Emily said, "Maybe Lorelai will know how to get in touch with them. Everyone seems to know everyone in these small towns."

"If only a psychic can contact them, I'll be more than a bit concerned. That would mean they are..." Tyler said, sliding Emily a sly glance.

"They're not dead!" Emily interrupted, trying not to grin, but adding more seriously: "You've become so pessimistic lately."

"Well, if I expect the worst, and the worst doesn't happen, then I'm better off," Tyler stated, quickly putting up his usual barrier against all anxieties.

"So... what about food? I'm sure this parking lot will lose its glamor after the first day or two of just sitting here." she said, trying to turn the conversation.

"Ok. Let's just do pizza. I'll order from my phone, and we can pick it up on the way back to the house," Tyler replied. "What do you like?"

"I'm not picky. Just no anchovies," Emily replied, edging the car out of the parking space.

Tyler noticed enviously that she expertly maneuvered the car out of the tightest spot in the entire parking lot. Losing the battle within of "Do I keep my mouth shut or do I say something?" He opened his mouth and the words just spewed. "Wait a minute. You can back out of this parking space like a pro, but you won't eat anchovies?"

"Tyler, what does one have to do with the other?" Emily questioned, although knowing Tyler and his flippancy, she was sure there was some kind of connection in his brain.

"Well, you see… backing out of a tight parking space is kind of scary. And the thought of eating anchovies is kind of scary…" Tyler chuckled at his comparison while pulling up the web page for Domino's on his phone and selecting the one nearest to the house.

Emily chuckled along with him as if she understood what he was talking about. She felt it best to just go along at this point.

Once the webpage fully loaded, he ordered a medium deluxe pizza for Emily, a medium meat lover for himself and a couple of drinks for pick up. He plugged the address into Emily's GPS and sat back thinking about everything they had just learned at the library. He had a strong intuition that the chief of police had something to do with that accident in 1962. There wouldn't be any way to prove it unless someone confessed. Even if they ended up involving the psychic somehow, and there was confirmation from an otherworldly spirit, it wouldn't be enough to stand against such a pillar of the community - a decorated and highly respected police officer, no less.

They rode in silence most of the way to Domino's. Emily was still reminiscing about her past, and while Tyler remained deep in thought, saying nothing, she still talked on. Maybe she just needed to vent. Approaching the restaurant, Emily, once again, pulled perfectly into the carpark. She went inside to pick up their order, coming out with her hands full. Tyler jumped out of the car to assist her. He knew he should have gone in with her, but instead he stayed in the car staring at his phone.

"That was easy," Tyler said.

"For you maybe," Emily said, wryly musing that him carrying the pizza boxes for about two yards didn't amount to much actual help. "Let's get back to the house. It's almost dark now, and I'm curious to see if lights are on and beds are made."

Night Four

Thursday October 28, 2021

Upon entering the driveway - the sun vanishing behind the tree line - they saw the porch lights were still on. They gathered their belongings, and with pizza boxes in hand, walked up the brick steps to the front door. Emily checked it first to see if it would open on its own and was relieved when she had to reach into her purse to dig out the key. The hallway light was no longer burning, but when they took a quick peek into Tyler's room, something was wrong - or at least not as they expected. The bedspread had been removed from the back of the couch and used to remake the bed.

"Someone's been in this house," Tyler said, stating the obvious. With a tiny flare up of bravado he added: "Unless we have a particular houseproud poltergeist."

Emily ignored his flippancy. He was getting used to that. She said, with an edge of concern: "I think you're right." While Tyler quickly checked the downstairs rooms for anything out of the ordinary, she pulled out her phone to check for any missed calls or messages, but then remembered the sound had been on the whole time. She would have heard any attempt to contact her. Her next thought was to see if the cameras were all still working. Walking towards the back of the house, she placed her things on the dining room table and dropped her pizza off at the kitchen counter. Tyler followed. She checked the power to the DVR box and noticed it was still on. They quickly checked out the upstairs rooms, finding nothing out of the ordinary.

Coming down into the hallway, they noticed the cupboard door was once more slightly ajar. Feeling rather brave, Tyler pulled it open enough to poke his head in. "Harry? You in there?" he asked to the void of the small closet. Emily shook her head. How old was he - twelve? She kept her mouth shut. Best not to react. They closed the door, figuring their weight on the stairs had somehow caused the door to swing open itself. Back in the kitchen, they set the pizza on a plate - in an attempt at being civilized - and sat facing the DVR monitor.

"Let's rewind this footage and see what's going on in here while we were out," Emily suggested.

"I think that's a great idea," Tyler replied.

They rewound to just before Emily left for the library.

Knowing they didn't have another seven or eight hours to sit and watch the entire playback, Emily increased the speed by three times. Though there was no movement on the camera screens, time was flying by on the playback counter. Nothing exciting - Zilch.

"Wait! Who's that?" Emily suddenly exclaimed, with an unladylike spray of pizza crumbs.

"I have no freakin' clue. What the… How did she even…" Tyler said, barely able to spit out a complete sentence.

The image on the screen was that of a person - apparently female - walking about the house. Her face was obscured with a mask, like the ubiquitous covid ones. Other than her general feminine hair and body shape she had no distinct features. She moved from room to room as if searching the whole house. But what for? And who was she?

"How did she get in this house? No one came through the front door!" Tyler finally exploded, unable to keep his excitement in any longer.

"I don't know. I can't see any facial features because of the mask," Emily said, expertly keeping a lid on her own rising anticipation, "I have no clue how she got in. Maybe she's one of the ghosts?"

"That's one solid and clear apparition if that's a ghost," Tyler replied, "I've only seen something like that once in my life, but thinking back, it was still slightly see through. Let's just face it, she's an intruder. Maybe even a murderer - who knows? I think we should call the cops."

"Murderer? Really? Now you're jumping to conclusions," Emily responded, having enough of his wild assumptions.

"Hold on just a moment. Let's keep watching and see what she does."

The mystery lady moved across the living room after entering the camera frame - which was cut off just before the closet - and picked up the comforter from the back of the couch. On another camera she could be seen moving across the hallway, and the next picked her up entering Tyler's room. They watched her make the bed to the pristine condition they had found upon returning home. Then she exited the room.

"Did you see that?" Tyler asked, "There was something in her hands. What was that?"

"No. I didn't. Let's get a better look," Emily responded.

Zooming in turned the image grainy and pixelated, making it hard to tell what the mysterious woman was holding. Whatever it was, they watched her place it in the cupboard beneath the stairs. Afterward, she went upstairs to the library, where she began to browse through one of the bookcases.

"Pause this!" Tyler said, rushing back over to the cupboard.

Emily used the mouse to click on the "Pause" icon and followed him. Opening the cupboard, the only thing found inside was a poker that appeared to match the set from the living room fireplace. They hadn't paid much attention to the fireplace, except when they arrived, so they had no way of knowing whether that was the same poker that was now in the cupboard. Tyler remarked he didn't remember noticing it when he looked in shortly before his lame Harry Potter gag.

They ran upstairs and into the library where the surveillance footage had shown the lady standing at one of the bookcases - and Emily knew exactly which one. It was the very one where she had found the Nichols book. She wondered if the intruder was looking for it but noticed it was gone?

"This is interesting," she said to Tyler. "This is the same case where I found the Nichols book. What was she doing? Was she looking for it?"

"We didn't finish the video before she walked away," Tyler replied, "I wonder if there was something particular she was looking for? Do the amenities listed on the Airbnb app mention anything about a daily housekeeper?"

"I don't remember, and my phone is downstairs," Emily answered, "But I don't notice anything different in this bookcase from this morning. Let's go back downstairs and see what happens next."

"Sounds like a plan," Tyler said, "Speaking of plans, at what point do we call the cops?" He was determined to remind her of the potential danger - not from the otherworld but very much from this one.

"Not yet. We need to figure out what's going on first," Emily said, cutting Tyler a sharp look. "Besides, isn't it you who thinks the police force here is corrupt?"

"That's not fair," Tyler hit back, "I'm just worried about our safety right now."

Emily glared at him and then walked back downstairs to the kitchen. Of course, she was concerned about their safety. She just wasn't ready to get the cops involved. Tossing her head a little petulantly, she resumed the playback, watching the lady standing at the bookcase for what seemed like seconds though in real time it was close to five minutes. The mystery woman ran her index finger across each row until she stopped at the place where Emily had removed the Nichols book, then turned and left the room. The new hallway camera that they had set up to cover the door to Emily's room picked up the intruder coming out of the library, but she disappeared just out of view and was never seen coming down the stairs. Emily scanned through all the cameras, but she was nowhere to be found. She had gone just as quickly and mysteriously as she had appeared.

"What the hell?" Tyler was baffled, but still remembered not to tweak the hair on the top of his head as he often did when puzzled. (Someone had told him he looked like Stan Laurel of Laurel and Hardy fame.)

"Now you see why I don't want to go to the police," Emily said, "because we have no clue how she got in or out of here. We're not even sure that's a living person. A living person can't just appear and disappear inside a house."

"That is true," Tyler said, keen to be seen to agree. But hey, if things got any crazier, he was heading back to Winston at Mach speed.

Emily stopped the playback when she watched the two of them enter the front door with pizzas in hand. She reset the cameras to resume recording, and they finished off their dinner. It was now time to get set up for tonight's investigation. Things were so hectic that she hadn't taken the time to plan tonight's investigation. Not a first, but this would be one of the few exceptions where they'd just have to wing it. She suggested to Tyler that they split up - one to cover the upstairs and the other the downstairs. They would stay in each spot for roughly thirty minutes, then they would change locations. They could even alternate on investigating inside and outside the house.

Tyler wasn't very happy about this but decided not to push the issue. He would see how things went. In a normal investigation he'd love to try this - but nothing about this place appeared normal. He chose to start on the first floor, mainly because if something got out of control, he could run out the door and straight to his car. He prepared himself to investigate the kitchen first, since they'd almost constantly heard noises and voices from the area throughout the previous nights. Making sure he had everything he needed - dowsing rods, digital recorder, camcorder and a spirit box and headphones - Tyler sat down at the counter fully prepared not to move for the next thirty minutes.

Emily decided to start in the library, wanting answers about the woman who mysteriously vanished after leaving it. She brought along identical equipment that Tyler set aside to use, methodically laying each piece on the center table between the two chairs. She started with the spirit box, a radio that plays a constant sweep of white noise through AM and FM frequencies. Emily intended to use it to communicate with the spirits by asking questions and listening for answers through her headphones. She would write down any replies she felt had been conveyed through the manipulated white noise. She closed the door to minimize any interference that might affect Tyler's investigation and sat down on the floor. After securing the headphones properly over her ears, she turned on the spirit box and - taking a deep breath - introduced herself.

"Hello, my name is Emily. If anyone is here with me tonight, can you please tell me your name?"

The sound of white noise filled her ears.

"Is Carol with me tonight?"

There was a skip between stations in the white noise and a scratchy voice was heard saying "No."

"Can you tell me who is with me if it is not Carol?"

No reply.

"I can't help you if you don't tell me who you are..."

She was almost positive she heard a reply.

"I think I heard you, but I couldn't make it out. Can you please repeat that for me?"

More audible than the last time, she heard a raspy digitized voice come through saying "Get."

"I heard 'get.' Is there something you need me to get for you?"

Another response came through the earphones, though it definitely wasn't what she wanted to hear. "*Out.*"

"Get out? I'm sorry. I'm not going to do that. Why do you want me or us to get out?"

Other than the white noise, there was no discernible

communication, but Emily had a sudden feeling that something was approaching her. The hairs on the back of her neck began to rise, but although she was becoming distinctly uncomfortable, she stood her ground and spoke out into the room.

"I'm not going to leave if you can't tell me why I should go in the first place."

A few more skips between the radio station sweep and the digitized voice appeared again. "Run."

"I'm not afraid of you. You can't scare me into running away…" Emily paused to regain her composure. Never a good thing to antagonize the spirits. Using a softer tone, she asked:

"Can you tell me about the lady in the room earlier?"

Silence.

"What was her name? How did she get in here?"

Emily sat on the floor, hoping for a response. She waited longer between questions this time in hopes she would either hear something from the spirit box or that her digital recorder might pick something up.

The static of the white noise intensified, and the

digital voice let out another distinct word. "Death."

Emily removed her earphones. "What was that supposed to mean?" she thought. She was tempted to let the rising excitement at getting *something* recorded interfere with her professionalism but shook herself and started to think objectively. What, exactly, had they got? Whatever was communicating had a very dark way of conveying information. She checked her watch and noticed that her allotted time in this room was almost up. She jotted down a few notes before reaching out to Tyler on the walkie.

Tyler sat at the kitchen island watching Emily on the surveillance monitor. He turned on the audio recorder and sat in silence. He could see her getting positioned to start her investigation. Beginning with a real time EVP session, Tyler began to ask questions in the empty room.

"Hi, my name is Tyler. Is there anyone here with me this evening?"

Tyler waited a good thirty seconds before asking the

next question. While he waited, he watched the monitor showing Emily sitting on the floor of the library.

"Andrew, can you tell me what happened to your car on the night of the accident?"

Silence

"Was it truly an accident?"

Silence.

Tyler stopped the digital recorder and rewound for the playback. He listened to himself talk into the void, with apparently no one to answer him. None of his questions had elicited any response, so he started over again.

"Lilith, are you here with me tonight?"

Tyler waited again, watching the monitor showing Emily on the floor. Though this time he noticed her body language suggested that she was feeling uncomfortable. But then he stiffened, observing - with a jolt - that a grayish misty mass had materialized by the closet. As it started to become more solid, it became darker and darker. Tyler couldn't believe his eyes. This was an investigator's dream. Was he actually watching something manifest while Emily was conducting her investigation? He started to pick up his walkie to check on her, but realized she wouldn't be able to hear him with her earphones on. He watched intently, making sure to write down the time so that he could play it back for her later.

The screen flashed and he saw the gray mass emerge so close to - and behind - her, that it could easily have tapped her on the shoulder. And that was the most innocent interpretation… Emily seemed rather wary, shifting her weight awkwardly, but continued to appear ok. Getting caught up in what he was watching, he had forgotten about his own investigation. While he had only asked one question since the last playback, he'd still been recording while the events upstairs unfolded. He stopped the audio recorder and rewound to listen. An unmistakable word came through his earphones, though it only came through around the time the mass appeared on the screen: *Sullivan*.

Glancing back at the monitor, he noticed the ghostly image was gone and Emily was still on the floor writing something on a notepad. He watched her check her watch and pick up the walkie. He picked his up, expecting to hear her at any second.

"Hey! How's it going down there?"

"Pretty fucking fantastic!" Tyler responded, "You need to come down here and see what we caught on camera."

As Emily joined him in the kitchen, Tyler was queuing up the video to show her. He started to explain but stopped shy of telling her everything. He clicked "play" on the monitor and the view of Emily sitting on the floor began to playback. She watched intently as the dark mass formed and then moved over her, before fading away just as quickly as it had formed.

"Holy shit! That's amazing!" Emily exclaimed, "I had a strong sense that something was coming towards me while I was up there, but I never saw anything."

"I can't believe we picked this up. This has to be incredibly rare and great evidence!" Tyler couldn't help but add, feeling somewhat overwhelmed and awestruck.

Emily proceeded to tell him the remainder of her experiences in the library, and how whatever it was that she was conversing with came across very negatively. Tyler explained how he got no responses until the ghostly image appeared on the screen and even then the only thing he got was the Sullivan name. Checking time logs on the equipment, they determined that it had come through around the same time that Emily heard the ghostly digital voice say "Death," which also synchronized with the image manifesting on the screen.

"This is great! I wonder what it all means?" Emily questioned, "Let's get back out there and do some more. I think I want to take the living room this time. Where are you heading?"

"I think outside. For some strange reason I feel drawn there," Tyler replied, packing his backpack with equipment.

"Sounds good. Please be careful out there." Emily said, gathering her equipment and moving to the living room. She decided to grab the poker from the cupboard as they walked towards the front of the house. Looking over at Tyler, she said: "You never know, it might trigger a response from the discarnate entity."

Tyler nodded and exited the front door, sitting down on the steps to pull the digital video camcorder out of his pack. He turned on the night vision so that he could use the gray LCD screen to see where he was going. With the camera in one hand and the digital voice recorder in the other, Tyler set out to roam through the front yard. Keeping with the real time review of the EVP sessions, he introduced himself to any spirits that might be around and welcomed them to communicate with him.

"I just asked a few questions, while I was in the kitchen. If you heard any, can you please provide an answer? If not, I'm going to move on to some other things."

Tyler allowed a few minutes of silence, while observing the bend of the road. It was a quiet night and the skies were clear. The only illumination came from the infrared lights on the camcorder and the glare of the porch lights. With the luck they'd had already, Tyler hoped to capture one of the souls said to roam the curve in the middle of the night. Another of his goals was to connect with Andrew for more answers to the night in 1961.

He rewound the voice recorder, but found nothing

on it, and continued with his promise to start fresh.

"The other night my friend and I were out here talking with you all, and we heard the sounds of an accident come through our computer. Can you, please, tell me who was involved in that accident?"

Silence.

"We heard someone who sounded like my friend screaming for help. Can someone please tell me who that was?"

Silence.

"Is someone imitating my friend Emily?"

Silence.

Tyler stopped the recorder and rewound. He played the recording into the desolate night air. The first and second questions received no response, but halfway through the third, a very breathy "yes" was faintly heard over Tyler talking. He started the recording again and resumed questioning.

"I think I heard you respond 'yes.' Why would someone want to impersonate her?

Silence. He waited longer this time, hoping that he

wouldn't be talking if something responded.

"Can you tell me who this person is?"

Silence.

"Where is this person?"

Silence.

Tyler replayed the current session, anticipating more responses. There was no reply to the first question, but the breathy "me" at the end of the second made the hair on the back of Tyler's neck and arms stand straight out. He immediately wanted to know who "me" was. The response to the third question was there, but it was muffled, and he couldn't make out what was being said. He started again.

"Why would you impersonate my friend?"

Silence.

"What are you?"

Silence.

"Who are you?"

Silence.

The playback this time didn't yield as much as he'd hoped. The only response was to the first question - a breathy “back yard.” Tyler turned around, looking back towards the house. He was just out of range of the yellow light that gleamed down from the porch. He walked the tree line on the far right of the house towards the back yard. The closer he got, the more the glimmers of light dissolved into pitch black.

They had never paid attention to the back of the house, and Tyler didn’t know what he would discover as he left the tree line and rounded the corner. By now his eyes had adjusted to the night and he could make out the dark blur where the tree line met the star-lit sky. Continuing farther back, something substantial caught his eye protruding out of the ground. It was round with some type of roof over it. Getting closer, he realized it was circular and made of stone - an old well. The roof at one time housed the crank, rope and bucket though it was derelict now and falling apart. He was interested to see, though, that instead of the anticipated bucket, there was a wooden ladder attached to the inside of the well. He pointed the camcorder down the inside, to see how far it went down. Surprisingly, however, it wasn’t that deep and was completely dry inside. He decided to investigate this properly when the sun was up and he could get a better view. Time had run out. He was walking back towards the house when Emily contacted him on the walkie.

Emily stationed herself on the floor close to the fireplace. She laid the poker in front of her. Pulling out her dowsing rods this time, she calibrated them until each metal arm was pointing straight ahead. Her goal this time was to determine the significance of this poker. Was it in fact what the mysterious woman was carrying around or was it just simply in the wrong place? She started by introducing herself and inviting the spirits of the house to communicate.

"There was a woman in the house today. Was this poker what she was carrying around? Cross the rods for yes, please."

The metal arms remained in place for a moment then gradually swung to form the X.

"Thank you. Can you, please, move the arms back?"

The metal arms swung back to the forward position.

"Was the lady in the house one of you? Cross the rods for yes."

The metal arms stayed still.

Emily reached over and grabbed her recorder off the coffee table, remembering she'd forgotten to turn it on.

"I can't ask you this with the rods, so I have a recorder here, and if you speak into the red light, it should be able to pick up your voice. Can you, please, tell me how she got into this house?"

The silence in the room was heavy with accusation, or so it seemed. Like it was jeering: "Call yourself a paranormal researcher? huh?"

Emily switched back to the dowsing rods.

"I'm going to leave this on in case there is anything you want to tell me that you can't with the rods. Does this lady come here often? Cross the rods for yes, please."

The metal arms swiftly swung into an X.

"Thank you. Going to reset now."

Emily shook out her arms and repositioned the metal bars.

"Does she work for the owners? Cross the rods for yes?"

The rods remained absolutely still.

"Is she related to the owners?"

Stillness. Emily laid down the rods.

"Ok. Let's go back to the recorder over here. Remember, please speak into the red light on the device. Can you please tell me who she is?"

The room remained silent.

Picking up the rods again, Emily decided to go in a different direction and focus on the dark mass that appeared on the surveillance footage.

"We think we caught one of you on our cameras. Can you please tell us if that really was one of you? Cross the rods for yes."

The metal arms rapidly swung into an X.

"Thank you. Can you move them back, please?"

The rods slowly swung back into a neutral position.

"Does the spirit captured in the video have any malicious intent toward us while we are staying in the house? Cross the rods for yes."

The metal arms remained neutral.

"Thank you for chatting with me tonight. My time is almost up. We will be moving about the house, please, feel free to chat with either of us."

Emily stopped her recorder and picked up the walkie to reach out to Tyler.

"Hey! You ok out there? Time's up."

They reconvened in the kitchen, where they snacked on leftover pizza and discussed their findings during the last thirty-minute investigation. Tyler said he wanted to check out the well in the morning with the benefit of daylight. Emily was just as intrigued but suggested that since it was after one in the morning, they should try to get some sleep. The rest of the evidence could be reviewed in the morning.

Emily left her recorder on the banister - in case anything otherworldly wanted to communicate throughout the night - before heading up to her room. She felt remarkably safe since the spirits had reassured her via the dowsing rods that the strange amorphous mass on the surveillance video had no intention of harming them. Once in her room, she closed the door and crawled into bed.

Tyler stayed up a little longer. The brisk night air had roused him. He worked on adding the information discovered throughout the day and night into their appropriate Word document files. When his eyes grew heavier, he closed up shop and went into his room to lie down, but though he managed to sleep, it didn't last long.

Blinking, he realized it was the sound of creaking stairs that had jolted him out of his deep slumber. Reaching over to the nightstand to grab his phone, he noticed it was four in the morning. He thought possibly the sound was Emily coming down the stairs. He lay there listening, wondering if he should get up and investigate. When the noises continued longer than it would take to get downstairs, he tossed the covers back, and with his right arm stretched out, felt his way through the darkness until the tips of his fingers reached the light switch.

The light pierced his eyes, which took a moment to

adjust before he slipped out into the hallway. Emily was nowhere to be found and not a light was on in the house other than his. He saw the blinking red light of Emily's recorder on the banister and was hopeful the sounds - whatever they were - were being caught.

There was a moment when he thought his name was being called, though couldn't tell which direction it had come from. But then the distinct sound of scratching drew him into the living room. It appeared to be coming from inside the closet. On his way there he felt a sharp pain start at the tip of his big toe and travel up his leg, which seemed to synchronize with the sound of a metal rod clanging against various unknown things in the living room. He had just tripped over the poker that Emily left lying in front of the fireplace. He pursed his lips, trying hard not to let out every curse word that sprang to mind, as he hobbled the rest of the way to the closet. He stood there a moment waiting for the pain to subside before opening the door, shining the light from his phone into the dark abyss. "Why didn't I turn the light on before now?" he asked himself.

Illuminating the deep walk-in closet, Tyler could see the trunk Emily had once tried to open was turned sideways and pushed back into a nook under a shelf. Otherwise, it was empty - and, he realized, unusually vast. There was enough room for him to stand fully erect and walk comfortably from one side to the other. At the opposite end of the closet, he found a trapdoor with a latch, which he assumed led to a cellar, and old two-by-four slats in front of the door that lined the wall up to the second floor through an opening in the ceiling. Reaching down to open the trapdoor, Tyler discovered it was locked. The keyhole for the latch was rather large and a type he was sure he'd never seen before, yet somehow the shape still looked vaguely familiar.

Caught up in the thrill of the find, he had completely forgotten what had brought him to the closet. Upon remembering, he realized the scratching had stopped. The creaking of the stairs had also ceased, and there was no mysterious voice calling his name. It was just him - alone in a half-lit closet with a trapdoor…

Tyler walked out of the closet and quietly closed the

door. He caught a glisten of the poker sticking out from under the sofa where it had apparently landed after the run in with his toe. He picked it up, examined it briefly, then placed it back into the accessory's holder in front of the fireplace.

Lying back in bed, Tyler was deep in thought about the mysterious trapdoor he had discovered and eagerly anticipated telling Emily about it the next morning. "Oh wait… It is morning," he thought after realizing it was now close to five. He closed his eyes, trying to find a way to shut down his mind. His breathing slowed and he was almost asleep when it hit him. He knew what unlocked the latch on the trapdoor.

Day Five

Friday October 29, 2021

Emily awoke the next morning feeling more rejuvenated than she had all week. She came down the stairs ready to take on the day. Grabbing her recorder off the banister on the way down, she glided into the kitchen to start the coffee. As Tyler was still sleeping, she decided to start working on the evidence review from the night before. Starting the playback on the DVR, she sat expectantly in front of the monitor. The events of last night played out before her, though aside from the mysterious dark mass they were already aware of, nothing paranormal caught her eye.

The house appeared to be quiet in the video until

she saw Tyler get out of the bed and turn the light on. She followed his every move from camera to camera as he cautiously sidled from the bedroom to the hallway and then into the living room. Since the surveillance camera had no audio, she couldn't hear what was going on, but when she saw Tyler stumble over the poker, she realized something important - she'd forgotten to pick it up the night before. She could see him leaning against the wall - just barely in view - when suddenly he disappeared. Sometime later she saw him re-enter the camera frame along the same route the mysterious woman had taken and eventually head back to bed.

Emily was completely puzzled by this behavior. What had drawn him into the closet? In any case, she realized the camera angle should be repositioned to show the closet door. She decided to do that now before she forgot. As she walked to the living room, Tyler emerged from the bedroom, meeting her at the foot of the stairs.

"Hey!" he said, letting out a big yawn, "Have I got news for you!"

"Oh, really?" Emily murmured, trying not to appear

too interested. She turned into the living room, heading for the camera she wanted to adjust.

"Wait. Why are you pointing it at the closet?"

"I was just reviewing last night's surveillance cameras and noticed that it wasn't in view," Emily responded, "Since the mysterious lady, and apparently you, have spent some time in there, I figured we should probably have it recorded."

"You saw all of that? Well, I definitely agree that it should be in view, because I think I may have found something last night." Tyler went over and opened the closet door, asking: "Notice anything different?"

Emily at once saw that the trunk had been moved into the nook. "Did you move the trunk in the middle of the night?"

"No, someone else did," Tyler explained, "But that's not what I want to show you. Come on, there's plenty of room inside."

Emily followed Tyler into the closet, only to be taken aback by how much room there was between the living room and the kitchen. She followed Tyler to the far end and listened as he explained the events of a few hours earlier. He bent down, pointing out the locked door in the floor and then the ladder-like slats rising up the wall.

"But it's locked," Emily said, as she noted just how high the two by fours went.

"Yes, but I think I can unlock it, and you're never going to guess with what." Tyler slid past Emily, exiting the closet. He returned shortly with a poker in his hand.

"Look, I'm sorry I left that on the floor," Emily got in quickly. "But you didn't have to drag me into a closet to beat me with it." She chuckled, "How's your toe, anyways?"

"My toe will live. But watch!" Tyler took the poker, turning it over-end, and tried to insert it into the keyhole. It took several tries before they both heard it drop and click into place. Rotating the poker to the right yielded no result, so he went to the left. They looked at each other in disbelief when they heard the locking mechanism unlatch. Tyler stepped back and opened the hatch. Beneath it was a ladder leading to an eerie unlighted room.

"Shall we?" he asked.

Emily nodded and turned on her phone's flashlight, shining it down on the ladder. Tyler led the way, dust trickling down each time his foot touched one of the rungs. Reaching the bottom, he took the phone from Emily and lighted her path. Standing by her side, he turned full circle, shining the light to reveal where they were. They both wrinkled their noses at the decayed damp smell.

The underground room was massive and spanned the whole length and width of the house above. They began looking for a better source of light other than the phone, which barely lit the area. With its only feeble beam, they searched each wall together - not straying too far apart. Finally, they located the switch on the wall opposite the ladder. The brightness of the dusty fluorescent bulbs hanging over them bore through the darkness, allowing them to see their surroundings clearly.

It appeared to be a vast workshop, possibly a storage area at one time. Workbenches lined the walls and various farming tools and equipment hung on the walls above them. Wiring draped across the ceiling, leading to an electrical box on the back wall. A long box freezer was tucked away in the back corner, with a puddle of water underneath indicating it had been defrosting recently. Walking over to investigate, they found it was locked, but emitted a faint putrid smell, which Tyler - thinking out loud - suggested it could be coming from the stagnant water leaking beneath it or maybe sewage from the large plastic pipe above. Passing by one of the worktables they found a chainsaw, complete with a full tank of gas and even a new chain. There was a dark brownish stain all over the pressboard table it sat on. Whatever had made the stain had flowed down the table and into a drain in the cement floor.

"This is probably where the owners store things in case improvements need to be made and stuff like that," Emily said.

"Possibly," Tyler responded, "But this chainsaw looks newer. And what do you think this stain is?"

"Maybe they needed some new equipment to trim the hedges before we came. It's possible the stain is oil from where they changed it," suggested Emily, after checking for dust by running her fingers across the top. "What strikes me as odd is this door."

"But why would they..." Tyler started to interrupt but realized he had been so focused on everything else that he hadn't noticed there was a door exiting out the back. "Right! Where does it lead to? Into the dirt?"

Emily eased over towards the door, reaching for the knob. Surprisingly it turned. They both glanced over at each other in anticipation. Not knowing what to expect on the other side, she slowly pulled the door open to find a screen door.

This opened out into what looked to be a short underground tunnel. The wall at the end had a ladder propped up against it. Tyler had a feeling he knew where this was going. They slowly made their way down the tunnel, when suddenly... BBBAAAAMMMM!

The screen door had slammed shut and nearly scared the shit out of them. They both jumped - almost into each other's arms - from the sound, until they realized what had happened - and it explained a lot. All this time the mysterious noises had been a screen door closing in the middle of the night. But who - or what - had been closing it, and so regularly? It seemed such a peculiar thing for a normal human being to choose to do, especially at night, that inevitably they thought of non-human beings - or at least no-longer-living human beings… The two of them wondered if the ghost had been opening and closing the door. Could it be heard from inside the house? Judging by the crash just then, it probably could. Composing themselves, they continued down the corridor. Reaching the end, Tyler knew exactly where he was. Looking up into the morning sun, he found himself seeing the sky from inside the well he had investigated the previous night.

"I guess this is our chance to get a better look at the well," Emily remarked, placing a hand on the ladder to check its sturdiness.

"Yeah, I didn't expect to be inside of it. This is all a bit strange," Tyler replied, wondering why in the world a dry well with a secret entrance to a house would even exist. "I just don't understand the purpose of all this."

"I'm a bit puzzled myself," Emily agreed, "Now the question is, which way do we get out of here...up the ladder... back the way we came? Also, I think we should investigate. I feel like we could get some answers from the spirits down here."

"I vote we go back the way we came," Tyler answered, looking at the weather-beaten ladder propped up against the well wall, "There's something else I want to look into back inside the house, and, yes, I think we should investigate. Maybe tomorrow, since we are going to the psychic's tonight."

Tyler followed the original path back up the ladder and emerged into the living room closet. He glanced at the two-by-four slats leading up the wall. Emily followed suit, not sure where he was heading, but could see there was something on his mind. Tyler exited the closet and headed up the stairs to the bathroom. Directly above where the slats would be coming up the wall, Tyler saw the bathroom closet. Emily entered to find Tyler looking closely- his head buried in the deep corners of the closet - directly above where the slats come up the wall.

"I think I've figured out how our mysterious woman entered and exited the house..." Tyler said, feeling around inside the closet.

"But there are shelves in here, fully stocked for that matter," Emily interrupted, not sure where he was heading with this.

"True, but they only go halfway down. Look at this." Tyler pointed out that there were metal hinges in the corners beneath the last shelf, which stopped just below eye level. The hinges wouldn't have been noticeable unless someone had gotten down on their knees looking for them as he had. They were painted to blend in with the wall. He gave the wall a forceful push and it swung out into the open area behind, revealing the two by four slats just below - ready for someone to climb down to the trap door.

"I don't believe it!" Emily stared in disbelief at yet another secret passage within the house. "You know, we should talk to Lorelai about this tonight. She may have some knowledge of why these passages exist. She could even tell us if the owners have a caretaker that comes by."

"Emily, think about this! If the owners had a caretaker or housekeeper coming in regularly when guests were staying, wouldn't they use the front door? And wouldn't they be on the amenities list or the guests be notified about it? Something's not right here. And speaking of the owners, where are they? They still haven't responded to any of your messages. You know what? Maybe they're criminals. Maybe that's why they're not responding. Maybe the wife is the woman that's coming in here messing with our things. They could be sending us on a wild goose chase for all we know. Paranormal or not, my gut says walk away. I know when I'm in over my head..."

Emily stood there listening to Tyler passionately pour out his concerns. She didn't have a ready response, but she knew deep down they were valid. They only had a few more days there, and she suspected that Tyler was talking himself into a frame of mind where he'd give in and travel back to Winston. She, on the other hand, very much wasn't ready to give in. They had obtained so much evidence of the afterlife and even correlated it to historical documents and research that she knew the Halloween night investigation was going to be out of this world, figuratively speaking, at least. She still wasn't sure that the mysterious woman had even been a living person. She could very well have been the spirit of a previous resident.

"… I think it's time to pack up and get the hell out of here," Tyler continued, "Emily! Hello! Are you listening to me?"

"Yes! I'm listening. I'm just not ready to give up yet. All Soul's Day is just two and a half days away. The veil to the other side is going to be thinned, and we are going to gather so much evidence…"

"See, this is how I know you're not thinking clearly. The day the veil is actually thinned is known as Samhain –the period between the autumn equinox and the winter solstice. It was celebrated by the Celts between our Halloween and November first. All Soul's Day is actually the second day of November. You should know this. You do know this!" Tyler continued on his verbal rampage. "Our safety could be at stake and all you're thinking about is getting the next big piece of evidence."

"I do know that. We would be investigating the morning of All Souls' Day, you nitwit. Don't insult my knowledge. But think about everything we have captured so far. Imagine if that doubled over one night! If you want to miss out on that, then whatever, but I'm not leaving. If you want to leave, then go. Leave!" Emily had reached a breaking point as her blood started to boil with anger.

Standing in the doorway of the bathroom, Tyler thought long and hard about the decisions that needed to be made. He wanted out of this house so badly. There was an obtuse feeling in his gut that something wasn't right, but he couldn't leave Emily alone in the house. Even if she had just called him a nitwit. If other team members were here, that might be different, but they weren't. As par for the course, Emily had succeeded in doing what she does best when pushed into a corner. She had added to his already serious sense of guilt for missing activity, not being a team player, and abandoning the team leader. Even if she didn't say all of those things, she knew how Tyler's mind worked, and played the game well to get what she wanted.

"That's not fair! I'm not going to leave you alone in this house and you know that." Tyler turned and was walking away when Emily grabbed his arm.

"Look, I'm sorry I called you a nitwit. As long as we stick together, we will be ok. Let's take the rest of the day and do some sightseeing. We'll do whatever you want. Take a break from things around here and get out of the house. We can review the rest of the evidence tomorrow. What do you say?"

Starting to calm down, Tyler agreed that getting out of that oppressive property would do them both some good, and there were certain things in the area that he wanted to see before heading back to Winston. The thought gave him a little relief. At least he wouldn't be in a house that someone could enter without them knowing. Nor would he feel the need to watch his back everywhere he went.

"Ok. But are you sure I get to pick the places we go?" Tyler answered.

"Yes!" Emily declared, "Let's get ready."

Emily agreed to let Tyler have the first shower while she piddled around downstairs. As he undressed, he stared at the secret door in the open bathroom closet. He couldn't help thinking that someone was going to come crawling out of it while he washed. And wished he could stop thinking of the terrifying and bloody shower scene in *Psycho.* He had the quickest possible shower and exited to dry off. The less time he spent in this room the better. Dressing speedily, he ran downstairs, alerting Emily that it was her turn.

While Emily was getting herself ready, Tyler took the fire poking key and relocked the latch to the closet trapdoor. Before leaving the house, they made sure the cameras were running and lights were on, especially since it would be late when they returned. Piling into Emily's car, they set out on an adventure free from ghosts. Or so they thought.

The first place Tyler wanted to visit was not far from the house - an old, well preserved one-room schoolhouse, which he had passed on the way in. The door and windows were boarded up, but there was a gray sign noting its historic significance by the roadside. Tyler walked over and read the inscription which had been impossible to make out from his car as he drove by a few nights before.

"You know, my great grandmother used to teach at a schoolhouse just like this one," Tyler told Emily, who was trying to find a way to look inside. "According to the sign, this is the original building."

"This is totally fascinating," Emily acknowledged, "I wonder if any of the Nichols family would have attended this school? After all, it was built in 1822."

"It's quite possible. Let's move on to the next place," he said, heading back to the car with Emily trailing behind him. The Nichols family was the last thing he wanted to think about.

Traveling the five-minute drive just off the main road, Emily pulled into the carpark of a large property surrounded by an old 1800's style wooden fence. The sign out front had identified the property as a fort. Filled with excitement Tyler jumped out of the car, leaving Emily behind, but encouraging her to hurry up.

"This is so amazing!" he exclaimed, reading the flier handed out by a worker dressed in period clothing. "This place dates back to the French and Indian War, though most of these structures are reconstructions from just a few years ago."

"It's remarkable they were able to piece all this together and rebuild it," Emily said, looking up at the massive wood building that had been recreated.

"It says here that it's built on the exact spot of the original from the 1700's," Tyler pointed out, "Could you imagine how much history this land has seen?"

"Oh yes!" Emily responded, "And - obviously - that makes me wonder how many paranormal encounters have been documented around here."

"The flyer says there's a small cemetery behind the office building in the back," Tyler explained, "It even mentions an unknown baby buried there."

"We should go and pay our respects," Emily suggested.

They walked over to the office, but there were no signs of a graveyard. Inching farther back into the woods that sat behind the antique building, they continued to search. There was loud commotion and Tyler looked over to see Emily holding herself up by the trunk of a large tree. He rushed over.

"Are you ok? What happened?"

"I was just walking along and tripped over something hard and almost hit the ground," Emily responded, pointing to a raised stone sticking up out of the leaves.

"Glad you're ok, but I think what you tripped over was a gravestone."

Tyler brushed the fallen foliage away, examining the moss covered stone. Its inscription had nearly been completely eroded away but he could still make out the "Here lies…unknown…" He noticed there were a couple more stones under the leaves. He was standing on graves: He'd found the cemetery. Emily hobbled over to where he was standing, trying to shake the pain out of her foot.

"I guess this is payback for leaving a poker lying around," she quipped.

Tyler chuckled but then knelt down, suddenly very

serious. They shared a moment of silence for those resting beneath them before heading back to the car.

The next location Tyler picked to visit was deep in Statesville lore, though it wasn't a location they could physically access. It did, however, fit right up their alley. The facts: A steam locomotive traveling 30 to 40 mph plummeted off the Bostian Bridge into a ravine, killing 23 people in 1891. The rumors: Every year on the anniversary a ghost train can be heard going across the bridge in the wee hours of the morning. The ghostly figure of the engineer has been seen asking for the time. Tyler, having read about this story multiple times, couldn't wait to see where this tragic accident had occurred, even if it was from the inside of a car.

Traveling down a narrow meandering road, he watched for any signs of the old train tracks. Coming up on a bridge, he raised himself up in the passenger seat and gazed out in anticipation. Since there wasn't any other traffic around, Emily slowed down as they passed. In the distance was the Bostian Bridge rising above a creek. Tyler grabbed his phone to take a quick picture and then relaxed back in his seat. After heading back into town, there was one other place on his list to visit before they headed back to meet the psychic - Historic Downtown Statesville.

Though they'd been downtown when they visited the library, there hadn't been much time for sightseeing, and the area had a certain attractiveness. They pulled into a parking space and got out of the car. Emily's foot was starting to become quite painful as she braved the hike along the sidewalks between the 1950's-style two-story shops. Tyler led the way past the green clock tower in the center of town, then south until they reached his researched destination. Standing across the street to get a panoramic view of the building, Tyler pointed at the desolate building and said:

"I think you're going to like this place," Tyler told Emily, "It's another haunted location. It seems no matter how hard we try, we can never escape the ghosts."

"It does seem that way," Emily replied, "What's the story here?"

"It's called The Vance Hotel and it's a historic

landmark in the town," Tyler explained, "From the paranormal aspect, witnesses have said sometimes when they walk by the hotel at night, a little girl can be seen at the basement windows that look out onto the sidewalk."

"That's fascinating!" Emily exclaimed, "Do they know who she is?"

"Nope. They say she just stands in the window and waves, then she slowly fades away. Sometimes witnesses don't think or agree she's a little girl at all. Some think she's a demonic shapeshifter, though there's never been proof of any of this. It's still a pretty cool location. Hasn't been open in years. Used to be a restaurant inside the hotel at one time. It's permanently closed now but would have made a cool location to investigate back in the day."

"That's pretty awesome," Emily said, "I bet it was glorious in its prime. Thank you for showing me all these fun little tidbits of Statesville. I've really enjoyed our day away from the investigation. It's been relaxing, well, aside from a jacked-up foot. How did you know about all these great locations?"

"I had a friend who grew up here," Tyler explained,

as they headed back towards the car. “I never made it to visit before he moved away. This was kinda my chance. How is your foot anyways?”

“I think it’s ok. Still a bit sore.”

“Hopefully, it will start feeling better soon,” Tyler said, “Maybe we should stop and get some pain meds on the way to the psychic.”

“I’ve got some in my purse, I think,” Emily said, sliding back into the driver seat.

With the sun going down behind them, they drove off to continue the investigation they had set aside for the day. Oblivious to what the night might bring. Elated at the prospect of answers to come.

Night Five

Friday October 29, 2021

Emily turned into the familiar driveway, this time coming to a halt in front of an old wooden barn that now served as a garage. Exiting the car, she felt a sharp pain radiating from her ankle, which reminded her she'd forgotten to take some pain medication. She lifted her pants' leg to examine the now swollen flesh bulging over her shoe - she must have really done a number on it when she fell. Not letting it get the best of her, she put her big girl pants on and plowed - slightly unsteadily - up to the door, Tyler, not knowing what to expect, hesitantly followed behind.

Knock knock knock…

Emily, attempting to keep weight off her swollen ankle, restlessly waited for Lorelai to appear at the door. She could hear the faint sounds of clunking coming from inside. When no one arrived, she knocked again.

Knock knock knock…

Tyler looked around the grounds - multiple open barns storing large farm machinery, vast desolate pastures that he assumed connected to "their" house, and a multitude of crows resembling something from *The Birds* - giving him a quick case of the chills, or maybe it was just the lowering fall temperature. Suddenly, something behind the house caught his eye. Backed into a shed was an old 1970's pickup. Either they were a popular commodity around there, or this was the same one he'd watched back out of the driveway just the other day. Suddenly, his uneasy feeling had returned - something wasn't right. He was about to point this out to Emily when Lorelai came to the door.

"Oh, I'm so sorry, dear. Bless your heart. Didn't mean to keep you waiting out here." She swung the screen door open, welcoming them inside.

"Thank you," they said as they entered the house.

Upon first looks Lorelai was an older lady, possibly in her late fifties to early sixties. She stood about five foot eight inches tall with a narrow body wrapped in a red and white gingham dress. Her thick black hair, graying slightly at the temples, framed her oval face and hung down just past her shoulders. She was the epitome of your average farm wife and not at all what Tyler'd been expecting when he thought of a psychic. His expectations centered around a version of Miss Cleo. He decided to keep quiet for now - observing - letting Emily do most of the talking.

"Thank you so much for letting us come over. I really appreciate you taking the time to talk with us," Emily said, entering the house. The savory aroma filling the house hit her full-on as she entered the kitchen. It was a smell all-too familiar to her and brought back a flood of childhood memories.

"It's no problem. I hope you like cubed steak and gravy. It's quite popular with the locals," Lorelai responded, as she set the table for four. Emily missed this little detail, but Tyler hadn't. *Four?* Tyler looked around the corner of the wall separating the kitchen and the living room, checking to see if anyone else was inside the house. When he didn't see anyone, he glanced down the long dark hallway that extended off the kitchen - nothing but doors to various rooms. Maybe someone was in one of those. Who knows? But that uneasy feeling was getting stronger by the minute.

"It's my favorite! My dad used to make it all the time when I was a kid," Emily answered, taking a seat at the small, round table to the right of the kitchen.

"Good! It's still got a little while before it's ready. We can sit down and chat a bit before we eat."

Tyler pulled his notebook from his backpack, ready to jot down any pertinent information for the next investigation. Despite his uncertainties, he wanted to make sure things were documented as best they could. However, Emily had one up on him.

"Do you mind if we record our conversation? This way we can go back and use it for reference in our research." Emily pulled a small digital recorder out of her purse and placed it on the table.

"Not at all, dear. I normally record all my readings and provide the client with a copy once completed," Lorelai answered, obviously relieved she wouldn't have to worry about the hassle of recording.

"I've never been to a psychic. How does this work?" Tyler decided to jump in.

Their hostess paused with her hand on a large cooking skillet, looking into the mid-distance as she considered her answer. She stirred the pan one last time before joining them at the table.

"Well, normally I'm doing readings on a specific person. I can communicate with their loved ones and relay messages based on what I hear or see from the other side. Since we're just here to talk about the property, I can tell you about the feelings I have gotten while being in close proximity to it. I never dare step foot on the land, though."

"I see," Tyler acknowledged, eager to ask his next question. "What stops you from visiting the house - or the land rather - as you've just stated?"

“There’s a horrible history of death surrounding that house and the stretch of highway in front of it. The spirits all seem to come to me at once, and it’s way too much for me to handle. Maybe when I was younger, but not these days,” Lorelai continued as she glanced over at the timer on the stove. “These days I like to focus on things from the comfort of my home.”

“How long have you lived in the area?” Emily questioned.

“Well, my family has been here for some time. This house used to belong to my uncle before he passed away - he left it to my brother and me. We had moved in after my mother passed away and took care of him in his time of need just as he had taken care of us growing up.”

“That’s awesome!” Emily was excited to learn that Lorelai must have a great knowledge of the area, but she wanted to confirm it: “So you should be fairly familiar with the happenings around here?”

“I’d like to think so. What I don’t know personally, I let the spirits guide me until I either have it revealed to me or I find out on my own. My latest research has been discovering the meanings of names. I'd be more than glad to tell you what yours means."

"Sure!" Tyler chimed in, while receiving a glare from Emily - he knew she didn't want to stray from the conversation at hand. But it had already happened.

"Write down your first and last name on a piece of paper, turn it upside down and slide it over to me when you're done," Lorelai said, getting up to retrieve a thinly bound book and a large opaque white crystal from one of the shelves nearby.

Emily watched as Tyler wrote his name - Tyler Drewitt - on a page he'd ripped from his notebook. She wasn't in the mood for his flippant diversions this evening. She'd given him the whole day. This was her time to lead.

Lorelai lifted the piece of paper, glancing at the writing underneath. She opened her book and flipped through the pages. "Ah, yes. Here we go…" she continued to read.

"It says here that your last name has a German origin. It comes from the name 'Drogo,' which is derived from the Anglo-Saxon word *drog* meaning…" she paused, gripping her crystal close to her chest.

Tyler was on the edge of his seat with anticipation, waiting to see what kind of kooky interpretation she would come up with. He glanced over at Emily, grinning from ear to ear, but it was obvious she had checked out of this conversation. "What, what does it mean?"

Lorelai swallowed hard, then said subduedly: "It means phantom or ghost."

Silence engulfed them as the words sank in. Tyler couldn't believe it. He didn't believe it. Before he could bring himself to comment, the silence was interrupted by the loud buzzing of the timer on the kitchen counter. As Lorelai got up to turn it off, he started Googling various meanings of his name - not something he ever thought he'd find himself doing. Sure enough, after quickly browsing a few different webpages, he saw enough to confirm that Lorelai's little book had been correct.

"Dinner's almost ready," Lorelai announced, almost anxiously checking the time on the stove - as if waiting for something other than tender meat - "I think we can hold off just a bit longer, unless the two of you are in a rush." Why? What was she waiting for? *Who* was she waiting for?

"Oh, no!" they responded simultaneously. Even Tyler was intrigued at this point, though he realized she hadn't actually provided any readings other than from a book.

"Miss Lorelai," Emily was determined to stick to the investigation, "Can you tell us anything about the current owners of the house? Are they in any way mysterious? Do you ever see them around? We've been trying to get in touch with them for a few days but to no avail."

"Honestly, I haven't seen them in a few days," she responded. "Probably just before you arrived on Monday."

Something caught Tyler's attention and he jumped in: "We didn't tell you when we arrived at the house. How did you know that?"

"Noooo, you didn't, did you…" she hesitated, then brightened up, saying quickly: "The spirits must have told me."

"Oh, ok." Tyler leaned back in his seat - skeptical - waiting for the next time to catch her off guard.

"Anyways, I haven't seen them," Lorelai said, picking up where she'd left off.

"We've done quite a bit of research this week on the land and the house. We're just wondering how they came to own it. The last family we found having ownership of the property was the Sullivans - aside from the current ownership. There's not much on record about what happened after that," Emily explained.

"Well, you see, the Sullivans never actually owned the house or land. The story goes that shortly after the Nichols' nephew passed away, the state evicted the Sullivans from the property. It sat abandoned for some time before going up for auction and being purchased by the previous owners."

"Wait! You just said, 'previous owners'," Tyler pointed out, glancing over at Emily - giving her the "what the hell?" look.

"Did I say that? Must have been thinking about the Nichols as being the previous owners, which everyone knows they were," she backpedaled.

Emily just figured maybe she was a bit flighty, as some psychics have a tendency to be at times. Hell, everyone is a bit from time to time. She immediately thought of Tyler and his off the wall Harry Potter and Oz references. Lorelai just got confused. That was all. Obviously.

"Look at me. I've been so rude," Lorelai uttered, too quickly. "Let me get you two something to drink. We have wine for dinner, but would you like some water?"

"Sure! I'll take some," Emily replied, though with a sinking feeling at the thought of Tyler and wine - or any type of alcoholic beverage.

Tyler didn't respond but wasn't surprised when she brought him a glass along with Emily's. He wanted to jump in and ask a few questions himself but needed Emily to stop blasting questions at her so that he could get one or two out. He pondered what direction he should go, but before he could open his mouth, Emily started firing off again.

"Mmm, thank you. How long has it been an

Airbnb? Do you have any contact information for them? Like I said we've…"

"Let's get back to the death of the Nichols' nephew," Tyler interrupted, deciding to take his fair shot at questioning. "I have a theory that the accident wasn't truly an accident and police chief Sullivan actually covered up the whole thing to keep the property for Lilith. What do your spirit guides have to say about that?" It came out too brusque - almost rude - but he smiled to cover it up. Not a great idea to alienate their hostess - and a potentially invaluable source of information. Emily shot him a look. He could hear her saying "Down, tiger!"

"Absolutely not! Chief Sullivan was a man of honor who would never do such a thing. That accident was going to happen whether he was involved or not. I don't need spirit guides to tell me that."

Lorelai's cheeks had two bright pink patches - indignation or even anger. He noticed her demeanor change at the mention of Chief Sullivan and Lilith and tried to point it out to Emily, but she was so irritated by his interruption that she didn't notice. He picked up his glass of water and sniffed it - not sure what he was checking for but checking for something - before taking a sip. His next question was going to blow the socks off both of them. He just had to wait for the right time to ask it.

"My apologies for that burst of rudeness," Emily empathized while giving Tyler a "shut the fuck up" glare that could have ripped his soul out, resulting in him becoming the phantom or ghost of his last name. "Do you remember what happened that night? Do you sense that the spirits of Andrew and Carol remained on the property?"

"I've already told you there are many spirits there. Not all of them have been identified. I guess it just depends on who you're interacting with and when, that you get to find out who they are. As for the night in question, I was very young, just a toddler. I do remember the flashes of lights and emergency vehicles everywhere, but beyond that, I don't have much more to offer."

"That's interesting," Tyler jotted something down in his notebook. This wasn't the big one he had lined up, but it fell right into place. "When did you say you moved into this house? After your mother died, right? When was that?" He felt his blood rising as if he was getting close to something big, but already Emily's cold stare was warning him off. Certainly, their hostess' expression was rapidly hardening.

"Young man, I am not on trial here. I understand you are skeptical - I get skeptics all the time - but please don't question my personal history," Lorelai snapped, a dark flush rising up her neck as she angrily ground up a few extra ingredients with her mortar and pestle before mixing it in with the flour to make the gravy. Looking away from the frustration on Lorelai's face, Emily took a brief moment to admire her cooking skills as she was adding a bit of this and a bit of that - as if she had done this hundreds of times, which she probably had. She was quickly jerked back into reality when Tyler continued his interrogation.

"I'm sorry, Ma'am. I just don't understand how you would have been in the area as a toddler if you didn't move here until after your mom had passed. I'm just asking what year that was."

"Well, I'm not going to tell you that. Again, I'm here to help you with the house, not my personal background," Lorelai snarled, very obviously turning her attention to Emily, "Miss Adair, if you have any more questions, I'd be more than glad to answer them for you."

"Thank you, I greatly appreciate that," Emily sympathized, though she was over Tyler and his form of questioning. What was his issue anyways? "I do have a few more questions. We found a secret room underneath the house that leads into an underground tunnel and comes up through a well in the backyard. Any idea what…"

"Shit!" Lorelai dropped her spatula into the gravy, interrupting Emily. She tossed it in the sink and looked out of the window rather too deliberately. What was she looking for? It was then that Tyler noticed she took her finger and made a small upside down cross on the steamed-up window. He wondered if this was some kind of religious practice or maybe she was leaving a signal for someone. He glanced over at Emily to see if she noticed, but before he could catch her attention, the once again the affable hostess said, "I'm sorry, dear. Why don't we continue our conversation after dinner? Hand me your plate."

Emily passed the solid white crockery to Lorelai, watching her heap chunks of meat and gravy over rice. The hearty aroma rose in the steam when Lorelai sat the plate in front of her. Emily noticed that Tyler hadn't provided his plate, so she reached over. "Here, I'll give it to her."

"No, thanks. I'm not that hungry," Tyler replied, the uneasy feeling in his stomach - at this point - causing almost unbearable nausea. Maybe it was some kind of intuition. Had he been right from the beginning? What took so long for the food to be prepared if it was almost ready to eat when they arrived? And he stared at the extra plate - who was this fourth person still to arrive? He took another piece of paper, scribbled "DON'T EAT THAT" and passed it to Emily. But she just balled it up and tossed it into her purse before Lorelai could see.

"Tyler, you need to eat," she pushed.

"I'm fine."

Lorelai dropped off Emily's wine, noticing she'd not

yet given Tyler a full plate of the appetizing cubed steak. She picked up the plate, piled on an overly healthy serving and sat it back down. "Here! Eat, boy."

"Oh, yum!" Emily said, taking her first bite. "This is delicious. Just like my dad used to make."

"I'm so glad you enjoy it. Eat up!" Lorelai replied.

"I notice you haven't made yourself a plate. Are you not eating?" Tyler questioned. "And who's the other plate for?

"I'm working on that now," she said, taking her plate to the stove, she loaded it with rice but added very little meat and gravy. She returned to the table with her plate in one hand and a bottle of wine in the other. She poured herself, then Tyler a glass. Tyler noticed she had completely avoided his question regarding the other place setting.

Emily, evidently savoring every bite, began to feel a little lightheaded. Thinking it was probably from the pain in her foot, she powered on. Maybe the food would help, but the more she ate and the more she drank the dizzier she became. Was the wine really this strong?

Come to think of it, was *any* wine really this strong? She struggled to set the glass down upright. Still, she was reluctant to say anything just yet because she knew Tyler would jump at the chance to crow about being right.

"You need to eat, boy!" Lorelai insisted, taking a small bite of her rice.

"Nah, I'm good." Tyler stood his ground; no way was he going to eat or drink anything in this house. He looked over to Emily - distress showing in her face. He reached over, placing his hand on her shoulder. "Are you ok?"

Emily tried to speak, but nothing came out. She felt the room spinning around her. Bracing herself on the table she bent down to reach for her purse.

"What did you give her?" Tyler yelled. "Emily! Emily! Come on! Let's go!"

Emily tried to stand up, but her foot injury made her ankle roll and she lost her balance.

Whatever was affecting her, though, she felt no pain.

"Come on! Get up!" Tyler continued, reaching down, trying to lift her up.

"SIT DOWN, BOY!" Lorelai bellowed, abruptly standing up as another person entered the house.

Suddenly it made sense to Tyler - at least as far as anything made sense in this investigation.

"You are the Sullivans, aren't you?" There! He had said it. He hoped Emily was still able to hear him. He couldn't tell if she was ok at this point. "You were the woman inside the house! That's how you know all this stuff! You're not a psych…" *THUMP!!!* Whole body reverberating with the blow, Tyler saw stars and for him at least, the lights went out.

Emily had heard everything he'd said and felt great remorse for not listening to him sooner - though right now she was almost totally numb. Her eyes - succumbing to the dreadful new heaviness - would barely open. How could she have missed this? Why didn't she see this coming? Had the thrill of the hunt caused her to be so blinded that she had lost all sense of reality? She opened her mouth to scream "TY… HEL…" but that was all she could muster. When she heard the loud thump, she managed to open her eyes, squinting barely enough to see Tyler fall to the floor. Her body was giving out - she couldn't fight it any longer. As her eyes fluttered close, she saw a tall broad-shouldered figure enter the room - and heard that familiar voice.

"Jesus! Lore, did ya kill 'em?" Jeb yelled, as he entered the room. "Wha'd ya hit him with?"

"He refused to eat and was yelling things they shouldn't have known. It was getting out of control, so I picked up the cast iron skillet and took him out. Where the hell were you? You were supposed to be in here. I put the signal on the window. I thought you were coming?" Lorelai bent down, cleaning up as much of the cube steak from the walls and floor as she could - it had flown from the skillet when she clunked Tyler over the head.

"I couldn't come in here. Ya know that. She'd ah known who I was," Jeb replied, throwing Emily's arm over his shoulder and lifting her whole body out of the chair. He needed her out of the way so that he could get to Tyler who was sprawled out on the floor behind the table. He laid Emily on the living room floor, then returned to pull the table out.

"Lore, gimme a hand here!" Jeb leaned down, grabbing Tyler's arms, he dragged him out from behind the table as Lorelai moved a chair out of the way. They placed the bodies on the floor of the living room, where he proceeded to tie their hands and feet together. He grabbed a roll of duct tape from a stand nearby and taped their mouths shut.

"So… whad'ya find out? How much they know?"

"Well, the boy knew enough to know things weren't so kosher back in 1961."

"Whad's that 'pose to mean?"

"He knew Uncle Seth had to cover up for you leaving those spikes in the road."

"Ah, shit, Lore. Ain't nottin' they coulda done 'bout that."

"They were looking for those new owners, too! And they'd discovered all of the secret passages."

"Well, t'ey didn't find all dem." Jeb grabbed a beer out of the fridge, sitting down at the table. He arched his arms behind his head confidently - still proud of what he'd done that night some sixty years ago. "So, when t'ey wake up, ya gonna tell 'em everything?"

"Maybe. But I should be the one to do it. No one can understand what the hell you're saying."

"Da great all-knowin' psychic... strikes again." he chuckled as he leaned back in the chair.

"We need to get them back to the house. Go outside and get rid of the car. Be back here in fifteen minutes. Don't be late!"

Lorelai tossed him the key from Emily's purse and pointed towards the door. "Go! Now!" Catching the key with one hand, he walked out the door. He cranked the car, backing it up a little before driving it through the back yard. He pulled it into an empty barn stall and concealed it under an ancient tarp. It would be good here until he had the time to dispose of it.

Entering the house, he noticed Lorelai had finished cleaning the kitchen, but she was nowhere to be found. He checked the living room to make sure the two were still unconscious - but breathing. They were. Good! He hoped they stayed that way until he could get them moved. It would be much easier.

Lorelai emerged from the basement hollering for Jeb as she entered the living room.

"I'm right here!" he replied.

"I thought you said they were married?" she questioned.

"It's wha' she said. They not?"

"No, you fool. Look at the last names," she held up both IDs pointing out the difference.

"How'd you get that?"

"It fell out of her purse while I was getting the keys. I'd already done a reading on his name, so I knew they didn't match. They don't even have the same address. Anyways, let's get on with it. I've got the gurneys ready downstairs. Help me get this one down first. She's the lightest." Tossing the IDs on the floor, she grabbed Emily's pinioned arms and hoisted her up. "Get her feet! Get her feet, Jeb!"

"Imma comin', damn!" They slowly dragged Emily downstairs, scraping her back against the steps along the way.

"When we get back over there, we're going to have to remember to clear out all their cameras. Apparently, they got a new system because they knew I was in the house the other day," Lorelai explained, as they swung Emily's inert body up onto the gurney.

They headed back up the stairs to grab Tyler, not caring if he sustained any injuries on the way down. He was going to wake up with a severely bruised knee considering how Jeb slammed his leg into the stair rail before swinging him onto the metal slab. Lorelai grabbed an already lit lantern, hooking it to the front end of Tyler's gurney, and led the way down a narrow pathway that ran from the basement - barely big enough for them to fit through. Jeb followed along behind with Emily, crouching low.

The dark narrow hallway stretched about a quarter of a mile and ran underneath the two properties. When they reached the end, Lorelai stopped a few feet shy, letting the lantern illuminate the screen door. She opened it, using its hook to latch it to the wall. There was a cinder block doorway blocked by a large sheet of plywood that Lorelai backed into with all her might. It swung open between two worktables in the Nichols' basement.

They pushed the gurneys through the doorway and into the basement of the Nichols house. Pulling two chairs out of the corner, they proceeded to transfer the unconscious ghosthunters to the chairs, securing each human leg to a wooden one and their arms behind them to the back of the chair.

"That should hold them for the night," Lorelai observed as she climbed the ladder to the trap door. She unlocked it from below and disappeared into the closet above - returning a few minutes later with the DVR box from the kitchen. The two of them pulled the plywood door flush with the walls and unlatched the screen door, letting it slam behind them. They moved through the narrow tunnel, heading back home, deciding to clean up the rest of the mess tomorrow.

Day Six

Saturday October 30, 2021

The immense pain throbbing through multiple parts of Tyler's body brought him to a hazy state of consciousness. His eyes took a moment to adjust to the darkness that immersed the room. Where was he? Why couldn't he move? Why couldn't he open his mouth? Where was Emily? Was she ok? Considering the state he realized he was in, he wasn't sure at this point what would be considered "being ok." Being alive could be considered "ok" even if you were tied up inside an unknown dark abyss.

Panic started to set in - breathing heavily through his nose - as he wobbled from side to side trying to free himself, letting out the occasional "Mmmmm mmmm" with each painful effort. The struggle and surge in his heart rate increased his blood flow, which only worsened the agony from the contusions on the back of his head and knee. He was starting to remember what happened to his head, but how had his knee been hurt? Maybe when he hit the floor after being knocked out?

Out of the darkness came a muffled but blood-curdling scream from close by. He recognized the tone and from the sound he could tell that Emily was also in pain. He grunted through his own tape to hopefully let her know that she wasn't alone. He knew she was experiencing the same shock and could hear her shuffling around trying to free herself - each time making it only too obvious she was in agony.

He heard footsteps but couldn't tell which direction they were coming from. A flicker of light emerged as the loud rasping of wood against the concrete floor pierced his ears, causing more intense throbbing in his head. A tall, broad-shouldered man entered the room carrying two large buckets. He sat them down before turning on an overhead light that instantly penetrated the darkness. Recognizing they were in the basement they'd discovered early that morning - or was it yesterday? Tyler had lost all perception of time - he quickly glanced over the room in search of Emily. She was slumped just a few feet away. Her chair was angled slightly in front of his, and as he turned his head towards her, he instantly noticed the blood-stained shirt pressed between her back and the chair. She turned to look back at him and locked eyes - he could see the agony - and knew they had to somehow get out of this situation. But how?

"Ah, see you're 'wake now," the man said, walking over.

Tyler sat in silence, trying not to shift as much as an inch. Carefully watching the man's every move. He didn't recognize him, but when Emily suddenly thrashed around and screamed through her duct tape, he realized that she did. It must have been the man who had stopped by the house a few days ago. That could explain his truck being parked at the psychic's house.

"Well, if it's not my fav'rite husband an' wife," Jeb

joked, getting up close to Emily's face. She could feel his hot, rancid breath on her skin. "Guess what? Ya lied, missy. Don't like it when people lie."

More unintelligible sounds emerged from her throat.

"I guess it couldn't hurt ta take off these gags. Nobody's gunna hear ya from down here." He used his filthy fingernails to peel back a corner of tape and gave it a brisk pull, taking a layer of skin and hair follicles along with it.

Emily immediately gulped in a desperate breath of air as her raw face burned, though it quickly faded compared to the agonizing stinging on her back. She started to yell over to Tyler, to ask him if he was ok, but as her mouth opened, Jeb took the palm of his hand and smacked across her face - reigniting the burn.

"Don't talk! Don't ya dare say a word unless I tell ya to," Jeb whispered in her ear.

He slowly walked over to Tyler, who was watching his every move and slightly amazed someone had managed to silence Emily. He didn't wish her any harm and was desperately concerned for her, but, after all, this whole situation stemmed from poor judgements on her part. Had she listened to him in the first place, they wouldn't be tied up and locked in a basement.

"So, wha's your deal, Mister.?'' Jeb inquired, hissing into Tyler's ear. "You wanna talk too?" He slowly ripped the tape from Tyler's mouth. "What is ya? Some kinda fairy?"

The four day long - five o'clock shadow helped protect his skin from peeling off, but Tyler was sure half of his beard was going to be gone. He gritted his teeth, trying to control the torture as each strand of coarse hair was plucked from his face. Brutal. Savage. He didn't pay any attention to what the man had said. He was used to casual insults and besides the pain was enough to focus on. As he took slow deep breaths to control it, a tear dropped down from his watering eyes.

"Stop it! Leave him alone!" Emily screamed out, as she watched her friend suffer - tears also running down her face.

"Wha'd I tell ya, missy?" Jeb said, making a slapping motion and giving Emily a sharp side eye.

Just before he could turn around to administer another fierce slap across her face, a petite older white woman entered from the passageway with a trolley in tow. She wheeled it over between the two of them, using it to bump Jeb out of the way.

"Go on! Quit harassing them. Least ya got the tape off. Gotta keep 'em fed and medicated till we - well, I - figure out what to do with them. Have you started taking care of the others?"

"The others?" Tyler thought to himself. He looked around the room, but there were only four in the room. Who are the others? Where are the others?

"Nah, I jus' walked in an noticed they was 'wake," Jeb replied, walking over to the long freezer unit.

"We've got to get busy. Lots to do before tomorrow night and I need things to be in order. And I need their blood."

"Blood? Whose blood? Our blood?" Tyler thought. Emily immediately turned to look back at him. The fear between the two of them intensified as they once again locked eyes. They didn't dare speak for fear of retaliation.

Opening the freezer, the pungent, sickly-sweet smell of death invaded the room. Jeb opened the door that led to the well tunnel for ventilation as he covered his own face with a N95 mask used by farmers. The freezer had been defrosted, which explained the puddles of water Emily and Tyler had seen when they first explored the area.

Jeb reached into the freezer, lugging out one of the two thawed bodies inside. He tossed the cadaver onto one of the gurneys, centering it above the drain in the floor. He placed a five-gallon bucket underneath one of the drilled holes at the end. Tyler noticed that the body was male and the uneasy feeling in his gut returned - much stronger than before. Vivid images of himself on the metal slab flashed before his eyes.

They watched fearfully as Jeb hoisted another male body out of the freezer, placing it on the other gurney and positioning them side by side. He reached up above the freezer to grab some pliable tubing that hadn't been there this morning when they'd discovered the basement. Emily cringed as Jeb pulled out a large pocketknife - cutting a small incision into the underarms of each man - after which he plugged one end of the tubing into their underarms and the other, he ran down the length of the gurney - through a hole and into the bucket now between the two cadavers. He then took another piece of tubing and connected one end to the jugular vein of their slit throats and the other into the two large buckets of paint thinner he'd placed on the worktable earlier, creating a siphon.

"Paint thinner does betta than any funeral home can," Jeb mumbled as he flashed his knife around - pointing it at Emily and Tyler. "You gonna end up just like…"

"What kind of makeshift embalming process is this?" Emily thought, while watching the bodily fluids slowly start to drain through the tubing.

"Get on with it!" Lorelai shouted. "It's going to take at least an hour and a half for you to get this done. While you're waiting, go get something to clean up this mess when you're done." She watched as Jeb walked out into the tunnel that led out to the well, returning with a water hose.

Lorelai brought the cart closer to Emily, "Now, now, dear. Let's take a look at these marks on your back."

Emily jerked away as far as she could. The thought of Lorelai touching her nauseated her even more, but she knew she needed medical attention, so she succumbed to letting her clean up the wounds. Since feeling had returned to her body, the throbbing in her swollen ankle had intensified and she could feel it pressing against the ropes.

Lorelai dabbed a little peroxide from the trolley onto a clean rag, slowly beginning to wipe the dried blood away from Emily's contusions. It burned, but she coped. She was tough after all, and her tomboy ways had taught her how to handle the clean-up of scrapes and wounds. She was almost starting to relax when Lorelai switched the peroxide for alcohol. The burning turned into fire, and she let out a scream of agony.

"Gotta make sure we keep it from getting infected," Lorelai said with a sinister smile. "You can live through this, you know, if you behave."

Tyler watched the tears flow down Emily's face. "If

you behave..." What did that mean? He figured he would be the next one she played doctor with. Finishing up, she shoved a couple pills down Emily's throat - ensuring she hadn't spit them out. "Here, swallow these. They'll help with the pain," he heard her say.

"What did you give her?" Tyler asked, flashing back to the night before when he'd posed the same question.

"It's just a couple antibiotics and something to help with the swelling," Lorelai responded. "I'll be giving you a few in just a moment as well. Just wait your turn."

"Who's on the table?" Tyler asked as Lorelai ran her hand over the back of his head - sending agonizing pain through his body.

"Oh, yeah. I gave you a nice size bump back here," Lorelai pointed out. "And that? Well...Let's just say you could consider them the 'previous owners."

Now it was only too obvious why Tyler and Emily hadn't been able to contact the owners. They were shaking with shock to discover they were underneath them the whole time - that anyone was underneath them for that matter. Anyone dead - murdered - that is. Tyler was intrigued that Lorelai was so freely offering information, so he calmly and meekly pressed on. The more answers he could get, the easier it might be to formulate a plan of escape.

"What did you mean by 'we can live through this, if we'...?"

"Oh, no..." Lorelai paused, looking up at him while kneeling to examine his knee. "There was no 'we.' She could get out of this, not you. A male sacrifice is required to complete the ritual. I've just got to keep you alive until tomorrow night."

Emily could be heard beside him letting out a wailing "noooooo!" and sobbing uncontrollably - not only for Tyler. She'd just realized that she wasn't going to get out of this either. There was no way they were going to let her walk away with what she knew. But it was Tyler's gut that dropped. It was like hurtling at max speed on the steepest rollercoaster, just dropping mercilessly. Dizziness started to set in again as the blood rushed to his head. *Male sacrifice?* WTF? *A Ritual male sacrifice. And he was it...*

"Oh, like hell you are! You people are crazy!" Tyler jerked back and forth in his chair trying to free himself from the restraints. But he lost all sense of control when she suddenly rammed a sharp fingernail into the raw bump on the back of his head.

"Now, now. Let's stay calm or I'll have to give you another lump on that pretty little head of yours," Lorelai said, patting his head.

"What…is… this… ritual?" he mustered, while taking deep breaths to subdue the pain.

"Every year, on Halloween, we offer a sacrifice to the gods for allowing us to keep what the good Lord has provided for us. Mostly, we try to do it by causing some kind of accident on the curve. It gets chalked up to drunk driving or crazy teenagers and goes unnoticed. It's not every year that live specimens just drop into your lap."

As he watched her untie one of his legs and address its wounds he said: "I'm pretty sure Jesus wouldn't condone…aaaahhhhh!" Tyler was interrupted by another sharp pain - this time surging through his leg.

"Boy, we don't use that name around here. You see... Many years ago, when people were settling in the area, it is said, my great-great-grandfather sold his soul to the Lord Satan to obtain as much land and wealth as he possibly could. The deal required a male sacrifice each year. The family quickly figured out - as long as we offered *a soul* - we didn't have to give up one of our own."

"You people are sick!" Tyler yelped. But the insult didn't settle well with Jeb, and he rushed over with his knife in the air.

"Not yet!" Lorelai scolded, pointing at him to get back to what he was working on - by now it was obvious who was in charge. She continued with her tale: "Just like your last name, meaning phantom or ghost, which you will probably become - most do if they die on this property - our names have meaning too."

She added a smelly topical ointment to his knee before finishing: "My mother's name, Lilith, is Hebrew for 'night monster.' She earned that title when she poisoned Mr. Nichols at the age of nine, and then some years later, suffocated Mrs. Nichols, when she learned that she wasn't leaving the house to her. There wasn't supposed to be a nephew in the picture."

"Is that why you created the accident? Well, I'm telling you right now! You're not doing this to me!" Tyler yelled out.

Unphased by his reactions, Lorelai replied: "Oh, I didn't. I was just a toddler, but Jeb over there did. He was playing with Uncle Seth's road spikes and decided to leave them in the road as a fun joke. You were right though; Uncle Seth did cover it up. Had to tidy up a few loose ends as well. You see, Miss Mathis didn't die when she was hit by that young boy's car - she was still breathing. He put a quick stop to that."

"You mean he killed her?" Emily had found the energy to chime in. "Like you're going to do to us?"

"Well, we couldn't leave her alive. After all, we have to get rid of *all* evidence," Lorelai responded, taking a handful of pills, prying Tyler's mouth open, and dumping them in. Emily, looking behind her, watching as Tyler tried his best to resist. Lorelai's statement also confirmed what she'd fear for herself - she would be considered "*all evidence*."

"What the hell were they? I'm not bleeding or at risk of infection. Why are you giving them to …" Tyler questioned, nearly choking as she poured water down his throat and before being cut off mid-sentence.

"I told you I had to keep you alive. You have nothing to worry about - for now. You took a pretty big blow to the head. It will help the pain," she said, as she ran her thumbnail across the back of his head.

"What …*gasp*… happened to the house after Andrew…?" Emily's breath was becoming shallow, and the medications were starting to kick in. She felt herself getting tired and the pain starting to fade.

"Died? The State took the house and Mama had to leave. It didn't happen right away, maybe a year or two later. That's when we moved into Uncle Seth's. Didn't exactly happen like ya had planned it. Did it, Jeb?"

Jeb stopped the hose he was using to clean the floor of bodily fluids long enough to respond: "Huh?"

"Nothing! Just keep working! Aren't you almost done?"

"Uh, I gotta notha thirty minutes at leas'."

"Well hurry up!" She ordered.

"That prayer meeting you invited us to…*gasp*…it wasn't a prayer meeting, was it?" Emily paused, giving her time to catch her breath. "It was a trap."

"That was completely accidental, my dear. Y'all were not supposed to be here. Jeb, here, was coming to get me. I'd been down here all-night prepping and was tired…"

"So, you're the voices… and clanging… we kept hearing… in the middle of the night?" Tyler asked, starting to feel the effects of the unknown medication. "That… was you?"

"Guilty!" She laughed. "Though I didn't think it was loud enough to wake you two. Didn't count on you being into ghosts - having recorders and cameras." Lorelai was busily cleaning up her trolley. "Which reminds me. I need to go upstairs and clear all of that out." Turning to Emily and patting her on the shoulder, she continued: "Unfortunately, *if* you get to leave, I can't let you go with any of that."

Emily's vision had blurred, and she could barely make out objects or people in the room. The drugged drowsiness was hitting her hard, making it tougher even to hold her head up. Drifting off into sleep, her body went limp and her breathing shallow.

Tyler, on the other hand, still had a bit more umph in him and decided to distract Lorelai with more questions while he desperately searched for a way out. He slowly shifted to gauge just how tight the ropes were that bound him, noticing that the one rope on his injured leg had not been re-tied.

"What…were you…doing…in…the house? Why…make…the bed?"

"A tidy house keeps the devils at bay. That's what Mama always said. You two were quite pigs. Couldn't have any devils around until I was ready for them. I, also, wanted to see if it would scare ya off. Again, y'all living for the thrill and all, just kept right on going."

"What…was in…the bookcase?" his vision was fading, and he could barely keep his eyes open. He estimated how many steps it would take to break free, run to the well and up the ladder.

"The bookcase? Oh, yeah! I did go in there. You see, I was checking to make sure one of you had discovered the little clues I'd put in place specially. The Nichols book..."

"How...did...you know?" Tyler was losing focus quickly, but still managed to make a mental note of every entrance and exit of the basement. He expected the trapdoor to be locked and running back into the tunnel to Lorelai's house would put him too far away from his car. Ugh, why hadn't he driven? But now he just needed to figure out where his keys were. Hopefully, they were where he'd left them.

"A little birdie from down at the library gave me a call to say that someone was questioning about the house. You'll probably recognize the name if you heard it. Sharon?"

"That...bitch..."

"Honey, you're struggling. Why don't you stop fighting the pills and just relax? Your friend there's already done it."

"One… more… question…" he murmured. "What… does… your… name… mean?"

Lorelai looked back at him before entering the passageway with the trolley "It's German. Like yours. It means I'm a siren. Someone who lures another to their death."

Lorelai disappeared into the dark tunnel and Tyler's consciousness faded.

When time was up, Jeb unplugged the tubes from the cadavers and flushed them out with the hose. He reached for the chainsaw, giving the cord a good yank and igniting the motor. The sound reverberated through the room, but the two ghosthunters didn't budge. "This' whah Imma do to you, fairy!" Jeb taunted Tyler, chuckling and waving the chainsaw around, then lowering it into the torso of one of the previous owners. Lorelai hadn't given him instructions on what to do with the remaining limbs and torsos, so he tossed them back into the freezer and sealed it shut. He left the bucket of blood by the drain until it was needed.

Closing up for the day - lantern in hand - he traveled back through the passageway onto the Sullivans' property. When he entered the other basement, hoping to relax the rest of the evening, he found that Lorelai had left him a long to-do list - mainly - belongings to be disposed of. He dug into the tin pail of items in search of anything useful before dragging it back down the tunnel into the other house. His plan was to keep it all together with the many other items like cameras, recorders, clothing, and cell phones, and dispose of it all at one time.

Exhaustion set in on his way back so whatever else she wanted him to do would have to wait. At least until he'd been given a moment to rest. Reaching the top of the stairs, he heard the sounds of distinct chatter and an all too familiar voice.

"What a mess. I can't believe you had to knock him over the head. I figured she would've been the one to give the most resistance," the owner of the voice said, throwing her head back and cackling. He knew just who it was and wasn't happy about it. One woman barking orders around the house was enough, but the two of them together would drive him insane. The idea of relaxing was out the window, so he briskly walked past both of them at the table, trying to get out the door.

"Come back here, Jeb! Let me get a good look at ya," the voice said, catching him just before he made his escape. "It's been a year since I've seen ya."

Jeb slowly turned around and muttered, "Hi, cuzzin' Sharrin."

"Did you play a part in the festivities last night as well?" she inquired while adjusting her sweater vest.

"Nah, t'was all Lore. She did it. I jus' help't clean up."

"Speaking of… Did you finish cleaning up the mess downstairs? Is everything ready to set up?" Lorelai questioned.

"Evera-thing's fine. Imma go work in the barn." He uttered, sliding out the side door before she could ask anything else. Even if he had to take a nap in the barn, damnit, he was going to get some rest.

"I gotta hand it to you, Lorelai," Sharon commented, watching Jeb exit the house. "I couldn't do what you do each year. I mean, I appreciate you sticking your life on the line for the good of the family, but I couldn't do it."

"My mother taught me well," Lorelai responded - proud of her accomplishments of the previous evening. "I take it you will not be joining us tomorrow night, then?"

"Now you know George will not let me be a part of this. We have to keep up appearances. People think we are good, God lovin' folk...well we are - just not the God they want us to love. Your yearly sacrifices make it easier for us to blend in with the overly zealous religious folk."

"Why blend in? All the people in this town are sheep. You know, we're not getting any younger, and after all these years, you'd think you would have figured this out by now."

"Oh, I have. But ask yourself this - how could I lead these people to you, if we didn't have our upstanding reputation? I grab the historians and researchers and hook them just enough to keep them from finding out the family secrets. And George - my dear husband - George is the head deacon of our church. When the supplies are low, he leads the religious sheep to you so that we don't have to go without - or the devil himself doesn't come and take our own souls. We've done our part."

"That's true, I guess. We all play our parts. Even Jeb has his role, though I have to stay on him sometimes." Lorelai glanced out the window to check if he had indeed gone out to the barn. She knew he was out there hiding. She knew her brother better than anyone.

Sharon hung around a while longer, chit-chatting until it was time to head home and put dinner on the table. As she left, Lorelai tried once more to persuade her to show up for the ritual, but she was not successful. Jeb would have to step up his game to get the house cleared, candles in place, blood spread, sacrifice into position, bodies removed and disposed of - the list went on. She couldn't do it all herself.

She opened the side door yelling out: "Jeb! Ya lazy bastard. Get in here!"

Watching as Jeb stumbled half-asleep out of the barn, she continued to bark orders which he let flow through one ear and out the other. The brief nap was just barely long enough to piss him off - he'd woken up even more exhausted than before he'd lain down. Whether she liked it or not, he had no intentions of doing any additional work for the evening. Whatever she wanted, it would have to wait until the morning.

Night Six

Saturday October 30, 2021

Tyler stirred in the confined chair as he awoke - groggy from whatever medications Lorelai had administered. Again, remembering the horrors he and Emily had found themselves in - not to mention the terrible promise of his own very imminent future. He immediately turned his head to check on Emily, but the darkness that engulfed the room made it hard to make her out. He suddenly realized that Lorelai had forgotten to retape his mouth, so he whispered quietly, not sure who else might be around.

"Emily… Emily… Are you awake?" He heard a light groan from his left side.

His voice got louder. "Emily! Wake up... Are you ok?"

"Wha... what time is it?" she mumbled, shifting in her chair in the vain hope of getting more comfortable.

"You must still be out of it. I don't know what time it is. My hands are a little occupied behind me at the moment. Are you ok?

"I... I think so," she could feel her head wobbling in a daze as she struggled to make herself more alert. "Are you ok?"

"Other than the fact that these people want to kill me, yeah, I'm fine. A little restrained at the moment, but she forgot to tie my leg back to the chair." He stretched his free leg out into the deep darkness.

"Holy Fuckmmmmm!" The pain from his damaged knee shot up through his leg.

"What? What's wrong? Tyler?" The concern in Emily's voice heightened.

"Mmmph...well...the pain is still there, but at least my leg's free. What the hell did they do to me?" he said, slowly lowering his leg. "What are we going to do? How are we going to get out of here?"

"I don't know. I'm still trying to figure that out," Emily responded, trying to examine her ankle as best she could - the blood flow being somewhat blocked by the rope securing it tightly to the chair leg. "Why didn't she leave my leg untied? Listen, we're going to get out of this. I'm not going to let them turn you into a human sacrifice."

"I appreciate your act of valor, since it's partly your fault we're in this predicament. If you had listened to me earlier and called the cops or just left all together, we wouldn't be here right now," Tyler said, closing his eyes to ease the returning headache. "But there's no time to argue over who did what and why. We need to try and find a way out of here. Hey! I know. We could try screaming for help."

"Don't be silly at a time like this. It wouldn't do any good. No one would hear us except maybe *them* and the ghost. We'd just exhaust ourselves, and we need to retain as much strength as possible," Emily replied, "We also don't want to get the wrong person's attention and bring them back in here… Wait, did you hear that?

The sound of echoing footsteps and chatter began moving about the house. They both quietened down to listen, but the words were not intelligible. There was a different tone than the voices they'd heard previously, which they now knew had been Lorelai and Jeb doing whatever it was they were doing - in the room where they were now tied up.

Tyler squinted to try to focus through the murk of the room. Emily could barely make out the shadowy outline of his face as she looked back from her chair. She started to ask what he was looking at, but the minute she spoke, she was quickly "ssshhhhh'ed" from the chair next to her.

Tyler couldn't believe his eyes. The slight glimmer of light that'd caught his attention had started to expand and was now almost fully in the shape of a full-bodied apparition of a young girl, about nine years old. It appeared to be coming from the hidden door that he'd seen Lorelai pass through earlier in the day. As it fully materialized, the glow surrounding the entity illuminated the room.

"Em. Do you see it?" he whispered quietly, not wanting to disrupt what was happening in front of them. "Man, please tell me I'm hallucinating or something."

"I'm afraid not. I see it too, but who is..." Her words froze as the vision became clearer. Emily had a strange feeling that she already knew who it was. They watched the being intently as it stood in front of the door, solemnly hanging her head down until her face was covered by her hair.

Out of the darkness came a loud, unrecognizable voice. It seemed to echo throughout the entire house. The name it called out sent a chill down their spines, and they noticed the immobile entity reacting to the sound - the first sign of animation they'd witnessed since appearing. It lifted its head, looking towards the floor above. The voice called out again.

"Lilith..."

They watched as the entity began to move slowly across the eerie workshop basement.

"Emily, what's going on?" Tyler quavered. He was fascinated yet shaking with fear at the same time. "Why is this happening now? I don't have time to sit here and watch this. We should be figuring out a way out of here."

"Ty, I believe this may be what is known as a residual haunting. There's nothing we can really do but let it play out. If this being really is Lilith, then judging by the age, this might be around the time that Mr. Nichols passed away. And trust me! We're going to get out of here, but maybe we should pay attention for a bit. It might give us some clues as to *how* we can get out."

"Look at her. Why is she walking a little then stopping? It's like something is blocking her path," Tyler observed.

"You know - I wonder if the layout of this basement was different back then? People changed the interior of houses all the time," Emily suggested.

They continued to watch as the being moved around - stopping in one place then turning in another - as if there were imaginary walls, hallways, and doorways throughout. Piquing their interest even more - the entity, now assumed to be Lilith - began to float above the floor as if being summoned. Its iridescent light faded as it disappeared up into the floor above.

"Ok! What the hell was that? Did she just float up through the floor?" Tyler yelped, looking over at Emily. He wondered if they were hallucinating. "Either we just had a paranormal investigator's dream come true, or she slipped us one hell of an acid trip."

"It appears so, but I don't know. Maybe there used to be stairs there. I mean, if the layout was different, then it's a possibility. And I'm pretty sure we just watched Lilith being summoned, but I'm not sure who by yet," Emily sat puzzled until the voices started up again. Still having a little fight left in her, she took this opportunity to give Tyler a stern "SSSSHHHHH!!" before he could even try to speak.

The voices were audible this time and they listened intently as the loud summoning voice continued in conversation with whom they assumed was the small being.

"Where have you been? I've been calling for you for the past thirty minutes!" the voice said.

"I'm sorry, Mrs. Nichols. I was asleep and didn't

hear you. What's the matter?" Lilith responded.

Tyler and Emily locked eyes with excitement, even though the fear of their capture still loomed large in the background. It's unlikely they'd forget it. But still, were they really witnessing an actual replay of a conversation that took place almost 100 years ago? They couldn't believe it, though Tyler remembered before he had left for this investigation that he had wanted to witness a residual haunting. Well, I guess this was it. Couldn't it have picked better circumstances to make its presence known? Why when they were both tied to chairs? They continued to listen…

"It's Mr. Nichols. I'm not sure what's wrong. He fell ill shortly after dinner," Mrs. Nichols replied. "He's upstairs in bed with the sweats. Get up there and put this washcloth on his forehead while I go find someone to help."

"Ma'am, it's 2:50 in the morning. I don't think anyone's going to be able to…"

SMACK! The sound of flesh hitting flesh reverberated throughout the house. Emily's mind briefly flashed back to Jeb's hand landing across her face.

Tyler and Emily were amazed at what they were hearing. The darkness of the room seemed to create a backdrop for an imaginary live action play taking place inside their heads that went along word for word with what they were hearing. If the time mentioned synchronized with the time in their world, then it was officially Halloween - and 3:00 a.m. was right around the corner.

Emily thought hard, trying to remember what she had read in the Nichols book. Did it mention what time Mr. Nichols had passed away? She couldn't remember. According to Lorelai earlier, Lilith had played a part in that. Were they about to find out the truth? The voices continued…

"Now stop your whimpering and get up those stairs and help him," Mrs. Nichols scolded.

They heard tiny footsteps pattering up the stairs and the sound of Mrs. Nichols exiting the front door. Tyler was amazed and a little perturbed that the perfect example of a residual haunting - repeating its events every year on the anniversary, but which just happened to occur while he was tied to the chair. He tried to stand up, hoping that maybe he could hobble around, but unfortunately, he nearly found himself and the chair lying on the ground. He wanted to get up and follow the being around, but he couldn't. He expected that others might appear throughout the night, considering all the unnatural death that had been brought to this property over the years - more death than they'd ever imagined. He shivered at the thought that he himself might be included as a ghost of the house if they didn't find a way to escape.

The voices started again. This time, a raspy man came through sounding as if he'd smoked about three packs per day.

"You did this, you little devil. I told her not to bring you into this house!" the voice accused.

They heard a door close, and young Lilith began to speak.

"Hush! Fever's starting to set in." The tone of her voice had changed. It was no longer a little girl's but that of a grown woman. "Ain't nothing I can do for you, and you know it. She knows it. Too bad she doesn't eat the same things you do, or I could have taken care of both of you."

"I be damned. You're possessed. You are the devil. I knew this was you and your God forsaken family. Ever since my folks moved here, you've wanted what's mine. Well, you're not going to get it. Tell me… How'd ya do it? How'd ya…"

The voice that was fast becoming ragged - the man was clearly struggling to breathe - could be heard coming through the floor.

"Just a little poison to get you up here in the bed. You'll be gone before she returns. There's no one out here to help her at this hour. Now, just close your eyes, it will all be over soon."

Stunned and appalled, they heard the rattle of the last breath leave his body. Then the house went silent. What they had just witnessed made them both emotional. Not only at the vision that was unfolding in front of them, but at the thought of them taking their last breaths inside of the house. Tears started to flow freely.

"She was just a little girl," Tyler broke the silence. "Just a little girl..."

"I have a feeling something other than just a little girl had something to do with that man's death. Did you hear how her voice changed? It was like a completely different person."

"Yeah, I did. I also heard his comments when that happened 'You're possessed. You are the devil.' I wonder what he saw at that moment. I wonder what we're going to see when that moment comes for us..."

"I don't know. Maybe the whole family is possessed." Emily said, adjusting her stiff and sore body in the chair. Trying to distract Tyler from dwelling on what seemed like the inevitable, she paused for a moment then continued: "Tyler, we're going to get out of this. We just need to find a way. Why don't you keep focusing on trying to move your leg around? You're the only one with a free limb at the moment and we can use that to our advantage."

"Excuse me, but that's a little easier said than done. You're technically not the one they're trying to sacrifice." Tyler tried moving his leg again - this time there was less pain. Maybe Emily was right. Keeping it moving would help.

She didn't want to add more fear and stress to his already high level of anxiety, but she needed him to understand that he wasn't in this alone. Taking a deep breath and releasing it she said: "Tyler, you're not the only one they are going to dispose of. They're not going to let me go. I know way too much."

"If you know this, then how are you…? Why are you remaining so calm?" he asked.

"I'm the team leader and it's partly my responsibility to remain calm in times like these. It's also my responsibility to get us out of situations like these. You know, it's very interesting how the mind works in situations of major distress. Some can remain calm and in charge. Others fall apart. If I didn't have another witness here with me - obviously, that being you - I would suggest that all of the events we've just witnessed were some kind of dream or…"

"I think the time to step up and be a team leader would've been to listen when I suggested we get the hell out of here," he quipped back at her - his resentment continuing to build in the back of his mind. He currently wasn't in the mood for any of her philosophical mumbo jumbo.

Emily paused for a moment, letting his quick jab sink in. "You're right. It was poor judgment on my part. I should have listened."

Reeling himself in before he went bat shit crazy on her, he sighed then suggested: "Ok. Taking a note from your book - you know, trying to remain calm and letting the mind wonder - why don't we do an EVP session? If anything, we can at least have a few personal experiences before they send us to our death." Just hearing himself say the words made him tremble.

"I can get us started. Should we try reaching out to Lilith?"

"I think that's a fair idea. Have at it." he said, letting her take the lead while he fought to keep his mind focused on getting the mobility back in his untied leg.

Emily tried to get as comfortable in the chair as she could - the ropes were starting to burn against her wrist.

"Hello, everyone. This is Emily and Tyler. We could really use your help. If there's any information you could share with us that can be helpful to us getting out of here, that could be great. I'd really like to reach out to Lilith at the moment. We're pretty sure we just saw her, or a version of her. Lilith, who forced you to do what you did to Mr. Nichols?"

"Lilith, can you get us the fuck out of here? Or Mrs. Nichols? Either of you? Anyone?" Tyler chimed in.

They sat in silence listening, but there was no audible response. Out of the corner of his eye, Tyler caught a flashing green and orange light that hadn't been there before. He watched intently, waiting for it to happen again, but nothing happened - until Emily asked the next question.

"Is anyone down here with us tonight? Lilith, are you still here?"

The lights quickly flashed again as Tyler locked his focus in the direction. "Um, Emily? This might sound strange - well, nothing sounds strange anymore - but I think there is a K2 meter hanging on the wall or something over here."

"Really? That's great! We can use it to communicate. I'm not gonna complain, but I wonder why it's down here."

"Probably for what it was intended to be used for, checking for electromagnetic waves. We are in a workshop of some sorts. They probably weren't expecting to capture a pair of ghosthunters who would use it to communicate with the dead. The dead they created. Let's see if we can get some yes or no responses here."

"Lilith, there's a light over here that we think you were using to communicate with us," Emily continued, "If so, can you please light it up again?"

Three of the green lights flashed briefly.

"Thank you. Lilith, that's great. If there are any others here with us, can you please use all the lights?"

All five of the colored lights lit up, remaining bright for about five seconds before slowly fading from red back to green, then going out.

"Thank you," Tyler responded, grateful for their effort to make their presence known. "Can you help us get out of here?"

The five lights lit up again.

"Great! How?... Not that you can answer that with some flashing lights." Emily scoffed at the thought. She didn't expect anyone to audibly answer her.

"Can you show us more of what has happened in this house?" Tyler questioned. "Maybe that can help us figure out a way out."

The lights lit up again, flashing feverishly until the room went dark. They waited in anticipation for what the spirits chose to show them. Emily stared in amazement as she watched an image appear before her. She glanced over at Tyler, and they locked eyes. Here we go again, they both thought. Tyler hoped there would be some great revelation as to how an undetected escape might unfold. A glowing image appeared in front of them just as the young Lilith had appeared moments earlier. Emily started to speak when Tyler interrupted her.

"Emily! That's you! That's the image I saw when we were setting up the cameras! That's who went into the bedroom! This is just like when Harry puts his face in the pensive for the first time in Dumbledore's office."

Emily, for once amused with Tyler's adolescent mindset, was glad that - if even for a brief second - his mind was not on imminent death. She tried to respond but nothing would come out. Her own mind was holding her captive at the scene unfolding before her. Was she staring in a mirror? Was this the doppelganger? As seeing your double was rumored to bring instant death, it was odd she was still alive - currently imprisoned in a basement, true, but still alive. It was then that another reverberating voice emerged from the darkness. And as it did, there materialized before them a shadowy full scene surrounding the entity.

Emily could tell right away that it was the master bedroom from upstairs, though it was very different. She only recognized it by the fireplace and placement of the bed. The translucent scene in front of them went into motion as the raspy voice called out again.

"Lil…"

They watched as the doppelganger walked over to the elderly lady lying in the bed, assisting her to take a sip of hot tea.

"Lilith, you've been so kind to me all these years," the old lady said, struggling to sit up.

"We ladies have to take care of each other," Lilith responded, placing the cup down on the nightstand.

"You've done so much, and with such a fine baby boy. I wouldn't have made it this long without you," Mrs. Nichols continued. "I want you to take the house. You're going to need a place to raise that boy. I've already had everything arranged. You should be able to stay here for a good while."

"That's awfully kind of you, Ma'am. Even after our families' differences, I'm so glad we could stay friends."

Mary lay back in the bed as Lilith moved around the room tidying up. Mary tried to insist that she come sit by the bed, but she kept on cleaning. "A tidy house keeps the devils at bay," she would respond. She entered and exited the room a few times, though they couldn't see where she went. Her apparition vanished completely as it left the room before them. Now back in the room, she held an all too familiar poker in her hand. She used it to stoke the fire and tossed another log on.

"Lil, please come sit by me. There's something else I want to talk to you about before my time is up," Mrs. Nichols insisted.

"Your time's not up, Mary. Don't talk like that," Lilith empathized, as she pulled up a chair close to the bed. She took Mary's hand in hers.

"Lilith, I want you to know that I know. I know what happened that night back in 1929."

"Mrs. Nichols I…"

"Don't talk. Just listen. Please. I need to say this. I know what happened that night. I knew before I called you upstairs. You see, I found the poison. A nine-year-old girl can only reach so high. So, when I found it hidden on the shelf of the pantry, I took it with me when I left. I had to protect you. I had to protect myself. But I want you to know, sugar…"

"Mary, I…"

"Sssshhhh. I want you to know that I forgive you for what you did. You were just a child. You didn't know any better. And you've been here working for me ever since. And you've worked so hard, honey, pretty soon you won't have to. Pretty soon I'll be gone and I..."

"Mary, there's something you should know about that night. I failed that night. I failed horribly."

"I know, dear. It's ok."

"No, you see, I did know what I was doing that night in 1929 and where I failed was that I was supposed to be murdering the both of you. Oh, Mary. I'm sorry... I didn't know we would become such close friends."

"I know that, too. And I'm thankful you and your family have allowed me to live as long as I have, but now it's time. It's time for you to complete what you were meant to do all those years ago," Mrs. Nichols said, letting a tear slide down her face. "It's time."

Tyler and Emily also were in floods of tears, watching as Mrs. Nichols moved Lilith's hand - along with hers - up to her face. "You have to finish it," she whispered, closing her eyes, and pressing Lilith's hand tightly over her nose and mouth. The scene slowly faded as Mrs. Nichols struggled for air, returning them to their dark prison.

"Oh my God. I... she knew... she knew this whole

time," Tyler uttered as tears ran down his face, plopping into his lap. If only his hands were freed, he could wipe them away.

"That's so sad. I feel for her. Imagine living your entire life wondering if every Halloween was going to be your last," Emily adjusted her body as best she could in the chair.

"Umm… Hello! Look at us! This could very well be our last, if we don't figure out how to get the hell out of here!" Tyler's brain quickly shifted back to their demise.

"We're going to find a way out of this," Emily comforted, though she wasn't sure she truly believed that, but she couldn't let him know that.

"You think?"

All five lights on the K2 meter lit up.

"They think so," Emily responded, nodding over towards the lights. "Tyler! Look! It's starting to be daylight outside."

"What? How can you tell?"

Emily pointed out that there were tiny rays of light coming through the cracks in the ceiling - the sun was starting to illuminate the hardwood floors above. She knew they were running out of alone time. It wouldn't be too much longer before Jeb or Lorelai or maybe even both returned to the dark basement. "Hey, spirits. We greatly appreciate the show of your past, but now would be a pretty good time to help us out here."

The lights on the K2 flashed.

"No joke now. We're being serious," Tyler chimed in, and immediately after the lights in the room turned on. "Y'all could have done that earlier."

They were starting to get excited at how the ghost had turned on the lights, but that didn't last long. There were all too familiar sounds of footsteps clumping around above them. Expecting to get another show from the ghost, they looked at each other wondering what was about to come. The night had already been a paranormal investigator's dream aside from being tied to a couple of chairs and death looming over their heads, that is - but they wished they could have experienced it on different terms. Unfortunately, their excitement quickly came to a halt when they heard the latch of the trapdoor unlock.

Lorelai could be heard barking orders at Jeb, directing him to each camera that Emily and Tyler had previously placed about the house. There was a loud clang as they watched one of their monitors hurtle through the trapdoor, smashing into pieces on contact with the cement floor. A pair of legs appeared, descending the ladder. Emily knew exactly who it was.

"Oh look! You're already awake! Sorry about that. It looked expensive. Was it?" Lorelai exclaimed as she made the last step off the ladder. "How was your night? Dark? Jeb should have at least left a light on for you. Where were his manners?"

Tyler wondered where she'd left her cart of medications. It must still be on the other side of the tunnel. Maybe she wasn't going to drug them up for the day. Or maybe her hospitality was out the door. He watched her nearly trip over the pail, spilling its contents all over the floor. Emily quickly recognized them as their personal belongings. Their phones, her purse and car keys, the jackets they had worn - it had all been in there.

"God damnit, Jeb!" Lorelai yelled up the trap door,

“I thought you said you took care of all this mess!”

Tyler immediately locked eyes on Emily’s phone that had slid under a worktable. Wondering if she’d also noticed, he looked over at her. They stared hard at each other, eyes filling with terror and with rising anxiety at what the day might bring. Time was running out. If the ghosts were ever going to come through, now was the time.

Day Seven

Sunday October 31, 2021

Tyler and Emily sat as still as they could in their chairs as Lorelai stumbled towards them. The impact of the pail must have inflicted excruciating pain to her leg when she had tripped over it, because they noticed she was struggling to walk. Tyler was especially careful not to move his own leg, hoping she wouldn't notice she'd left it untied the night before. They were shocked when she walked past them and over to the bucket of bodily fluids that had been removed from the lifeless bodies of the former owners of the house.

"Damnit, Jeb!" she yelled, "You used too much paint thinner again. All you've got down here is bodily soup. We're gonna have to thicken this up before I can go painting it all over the room. Get your ass back over to the house and bring me some flour from the pantry!"

Disgusted at the image her words had conjured up, they heard Jeb scurrying about upstairs. His heavy footsteps pounded on the closet floor. Emily assumed he'd reached the trapdoor when they all heard him yell down.

"Wha'd ya say? I cain't hear ya up here."

"Never mind, I'll do it my damn self!" Lorelai snarled back, as she marched over to the tunnel entrance, mumbling something about having to always take care of everything. Tyler could see the stress of preparing for his imminent death was starting to get to her. Maybe - he thought - this could be used to their advantage. He just needed to figure out a way.

They watched as she swung the hidden plywood door open and quickly disappeared into the tunnel. Tyler took this opportunity to quickly stretch out his leg - the pain was getting less and less acute each time he stretched it. He quickly lowered it back down when he heard Jeb coming through the trapdoor. He could see that his presence caused Emily to tense up, as if bracing for another slap across the face. When he got to the bottom of the ladder, Tyler noticed he was carrying the poker key. They watched as he propped it up against a workbench then looked around as if lost.

"Well, where'd she go?" he asked.

At first, they weren't sure whether they should answer, but Tyler was relieved when Emily spoke up first.

"She went that way," and nodded towards the tunnel entrance.

"Not talkin' to ya, was I?"

This time there was silence. Jeb's dark eyes locked evilly with hers for what seemed like minutes - though only a few seconds had passed - before he turned and exited through the plywood door, following after Lorelai. Giving him time to get far enough away, Tyler started bouncing around in his chair.

"What are you doing?" Emily asked, not sure if this was one of his stupidities.

"Trying to get loose!" he answered, "Did you see what he brought down? If we could get that poker, we'd have a better chance of getting out of this mess."

"Tyler, every inch of our bodies is tied to these chairs - except one leg. And where are we going to hide a poker once we get it?"

"I haven't figured that out yet. One thing at a time." He continued to move around, raising the chair legs off the ground, and slamming them back down while balancing himself on the one free leg. Emily could tell that panic was setting in, and she wasn't sure how to calm him down. Or if she should just let him be. Whatever he was doing, it seemed to work because she noticed the rope around his leg had fallen to his ankles and nearly out from under the chair leg. Unfortunately, his attempts came to a halt when they heard voices coming back through the tunnel.

"I swear if you don't get this right..." Lorelai could be heard saying. "Just a little bit at a time. And stir constantly until it thickens up."

The two of them entered the room. Jeb walked over

to the bucket and began sifting in small bits of flour as he stirred with a large stick. No more of his vulgar and derogatory comments. It was obvious she had given him strict orders. Observing his every move, Emily thought miserably, "Oh my God! These people are sick," as she closed her eyes, her face strained in disbelief at what she was witnessing.

Lorelai had returned to the upstairs and could be heard moving about above them. They watched as piece after piece of their equipment was tossed through the trapdoor, shattering against the concrete floor of the basement. The newly purchased surveillance equipment was the hardest blow to Emily since it hadn't even cleared the bank. She tried to shake off the blow to her bank account that was to come with the purchase of yet another system. Why was she even worried about it? There were much more important things to worry about. How were they going to get out of this? She tried the only thing she could think of. Since she couldn't verbally communicate with the dead - Jeb being only a few feet away - she closed her eyes. This time focusing her thoughts on Carol, and in her mind, she pleaded:

"Carol, if you can hear me, if you can understand my thoughts, please… please, help us…"

Opening her eyes, she noticed the quick flash of green, orange and red lights from the K2 meter. She took that as a sign that help was coming. She just didn't know how or when. She closed her eyes again to mentally thank her but made sure to add that sooner rather than later would be preferred. At that moment she could have sworn the ropes tying her hands behind her began to loosen. Maybe it was wishful thinking, or a figment of her imagination. Or maybe… just maybe… it really was Carol.

Her eyes popped back open when she heard wood hitting the concrete floor.

"Hey! Be still ov'r there, ya fairy! Or Imma turn ya into a bucket o' mush like dis one!" Jeb hollered out, raising his head from his mundane task briefly, before sifting in more flour. Emily shot Tyler a stern side eye. What was he thinking? That was the problem. As time was running out, he wasn't thinking. Just reacting. And, she thought with a heavy heart, pretty ineffectively.

Tyler, however, was completely focused. He was no longer willing to just sit there and rely on spirits to rescue him. They couldn't save themselves when they were alive - except for Mrs. Nichols who had basically taken her own life - so how in the hell were they going to save them? His plan was going to work. He just needed a chance to communicate it to Emily. She would understand once she heard it. And she better damn well listen to him this time.

Lorelai continued to work upstairs, cleaning out the rest of the ghosthunters' equipment, clothing, and any other traces that they'd ever existed in the property. As she was remaking the bed in Tyler's room - a task she had done multiple times this past week - she noticed through the windows the blue Honda Civic sitting in the driveway. "Gonna have to get Jeb up here to get rid of that," she remarked out loud. Standing back, giving the room one final look-over before leaving, she ran through a quick mental checklist of her remaining tasks.

Once the house was cleaned, she needed to head back over to hers to gather the candles and candle holders. It was already after noon and with so much to get done time was running out. She did one last walkthrough around the house before opening the cupboard to retrieve the poker. It wasn't there. She briskly went into the living room to check the fireplace. It wasn't there either. "Oh well," she thought. She would have to lock the trapdoor later. There was no time to go on a wild goose chase for a poker.

She descended the ladder, pulling the trapdoor close behind her. Making her way towards the plywood door she yelled:

"Don't forget to get the damn car out of the driveway!" Then she disappeared into the tunnel. She was feeling tired as she made the long stretch back into her basement. A nap would be good before the sacrifice ritual. She was starting to feel her age - getting too old for all this - and it would take as much strength as she could muster to perform the ceremony.

Upon leaving the tunnel and entering her own

basement, Lorelai grabbed a cart and loaded it with wrought iron candle holders of various sizes. The black pillar and taper candles were stored in a box, which she grabbed off a shelf and heaved onto the cart. The last thing she needed to locate was the torch lighter, but she couldn't remember where she had left it. She decided to find it later and proceeded back down into the tunnel.

When she arrived back on the other side, Jeb was nowhere to be found. She did, however, notice he'd cleaned up the mess of shattered equipment she'd tossed down through the trapdoor earlier, as well as the contents of the pail she'd kicked over.

"Guess I'm going to have to do this myself, too!" she exclaimed, unloading each of the candle holders and placing them in a spiral design across the basement floor.

"You see this, boy?" she asked Tyler, as she struggled to drag a tall wrought iron four-by-four with a base from a corner. Stationing it in the center of the spiral, she took a deep breath in and continued: "This is what you're going to be tied to. This spot right here is where you will meet your end."

She saw Tyler glaring furiously at her. "Ok...well... it's not time for final words just yet. I'm just gonna let you have a good stare at this and think about what's to come."

Lorelai worked on the proper placement of her candle holders before going around and placing the appropriate candles in each one. There were two candelabras on either side of the center focal point, which she filled with the tapers. The rest of the spiral was topped with the pillar candles. She grabbed the bucket Jeb had been working on and let out a rush of foul language under her breath as she struggled to drag it closer to the ritual area. Seizing a paintbrush from the wall, she dipped it in the now thick, floury bodily fluids and began painting circular lines - connecting each candle holder - making the spiral even more apparent. Leaving the bucket half full, she turned to Tyler.

"The rest I'll leave for you," she said, setting the bucket off to the side. "Now, where the hell is that Jeb?

There was no response.

"Oh, well. I'm going to get some rest before tonight.

Midnight will be here before you know it," Lorelai said, disappearing through the tunnel as she walked off.

Tyler and Emily locked eyes. Tyler could see the fear and concern in Emily, but he was no longer afraid. He had a plan - and a good one at that. What Lorelai hadn't realized was that she had just provided him with everything he needed to make an escape. He bounced around in the chair a couple more times until the rope came free from the chair.

"There! It worked!" he said out loud to himself.

"Tyler, what are you doing? What if they come back in here and see you've tried to escape?"

"Tried? Honey, *we* are escaping! I'm not going to sit here and just wait to die. If I'm going out, I'm going out with a fight."

"Ty, this is not the time to be a brave Mr. Bigshot."

"Just hear me out…"

Tyler proceeded to tell Emily the plan he'd concocted and how he was sure that it would work.

There were certain things he still needed to explain, but before he could, the trapdoor opened, and Jeb slowly entered the room.

"Where da hell's ya keys, fairy?"

Tyler sat completely still and quiet.

"I said, where's ya keys!"

"You should know! You have all our stuff! Where'd you put them?" Emily spoke up before Jeb went at Tyler again.

Jeb scratched his head and began rummaging through the belongings from the pail, tossing things around in a frantic mess. Tyler hoped that he wouldn't notice that Emily's phone was still under the workbench. It was a key part of his plan. They watched as Jeb tossed everything from the pail back out onto the workbench - dumping out Emily's purse, emptying jacket pockets, even checking his own pockets. Confused even more, he let out a loud grunt of frustration and said:

"I'mma have ta go ask Lore. She musta found em up yonder while she was a cleanin'. Damnit!"

They watched as he steamed off into the tunnel, but

as they expected him to return only too soon, Tyler continued outlining his plan when Emily interrupted him.

"Tyler, where are your keys? If they find them and move your car we're screwed."

"Don't worry about that. It's not gonna happen."

"You've become awfully confident over the last couple of hours. I'm starting to get concerned. Even more than I was before. Please don't do anything reckless and get us both killed before we can make it out!"

"I guess the brain does crazy things the closer you get to dying. Or maybe just adrenaline and fear is making it smarter. Who knows? Look, you said yourself that either way, we were both going to die. So, if my plan doesn't work then we are no worse off than we were before."

"This is true…" Emily paused for a moment to let his comment sink in. He had a point. The spirits of the house hadn't really shown any signs of assisting them, and it would be utterly stupid not to try and escape if the opportunity presented itself. "Ok, tell me again - where does the phone come into play?"

"So, it's probably been on this whole time. I doubt they'd have taken the time to turn it off. But there's probably very little battery left. All we need it to do is last for about a minute or two. Long enough for it to connect to 911 and allow them to ping the location from the call."

"Right! Got it! And the poker is going to be useful how? We'll have to lock the latch below us so that they can't follow us, right?"

"Not if we split up. There are three different exits to this basement - the hatch, the well and the tunnel. If one of us goes in one direction and the other in the opposite, there's at least a fifty/fifty chance one of us will make it out of here."

"This is all great and all, but we are forgetting one little problem. Well, a big problem actually. We're still tied to these chairs."

"Don't worry about that either…"

The conversation was interrupted by the heavy footsteps coming down the tunnel. Jeb was about to make his return, but this time he didn't even stop. They watched as he went through the plywood door and immediately up the ladder into the closet. They could hear him shuffling things around upstairs.

"Oh no! Do you think he found…" Emily began to speak but was quickly interrupted by Tyler.

"No! I told you. They're not going to find them."

"What if they just decide to tow the car away?"

"Ok! Now you're the negative one. Have a little faith. Besides, they don't have a way to tow a vehicle. At least I didn't notice anything of the sort while we were there."

"And when did you have time to check that out?"

"When we pulled up, when we got out of the car, and while you were waiting for an answer at the door. I'm very observant. When we get out of this, you should listen to me more often."

"Ha! Ha! Right! Let's see if this works first and you don't get us killed."

"Again, trust me…"

"Ok. I'm trusting, but you still haven't told me how we are getting out of these ropes."

"Ok! Watch!" Tyler said, standing up on both feet - though he was still crouched over like a turtle under its shell.

"You got both legs free!"

"I did - and in the process I also managed to loosen up some rungs of this chair. The more I can keep working at it the easier it will be to get free when the time comes."

The conversation came to another halt as they heard Jeb enter the closet and come down the ladder. Tyler lowered the four chair legs back down as quickly and quietly as he could, trying to make sure he was close to the exact same spot. Jeb spattered a volley of gibberish from his mouth - whatever it was it was completely incomprehensible. He passed through the basement quickly and pulled the plywood door closed behind him. They could hear him latching the other side.

"This is good! This will give us the warning we need for when it's time to act. We'll hear them unlock the latch!" Tyler said excitedly. His plan was falling into place and Emily was on board. Things were about to be set into motion.

"How much more work do you have on the chair before you can break free? We are running out of time."

Tyler stood up, regaining balance from his turtle-like stance and looked over at Emily.

"What?" she asked, concern trembling in her voice.

"Wwweeelll, I just realized my first plan for this won't work. I'm going to need your teeth."

Night Seven

Sunday October 31, 2021

"My teeth! What the hell, Tyler?" Emily exclaimed. Had he gone completely mad?

"So, I was just going to jump backwards and let the chair break with the fall, but then I remembered I'm pinioned back there and probably wouldn't be very useful with broken arms."

"Good point, but what am I supposed to do with my tee… OH… You want me to bite the ropes loose? That's disgusting. I'm not gon…"

"Emily, if you don't, this won't work. Now come on. Here, I'll just turn around like this and you can…

you know… bite down," Tyler suggested, positioning himself just so that the ropes binding his hands lined up with Emily's mouth.

"Jesus Christ! Ok!" Emily leaned forward as far as possible. She had almost forgotten the scratches on her back - but now they were burning with agony as they yawned open the farther she stretched her torso up and forward. It took a few tries, but they were thankful the lights had been left on this time. Trying to do this in the dark would have been an even bigger nightmare.

Tyler felt the ropes loosen from around his wrist. He started adjusting his hands, trying to use his fingers to assist her as much as he could.

"Ouch! Don't bite my fingers!" he shouted.

"Well get them out of the way! If you want me to do this, you have to let me."

Tyler held his fingers out of the way, and it wasn't long before both hands were free: Holding the chair in place he sat down and continued to unwrap the rest of the rope from around his chest and stomach.

"Ok! Great! Now get me out of this chair!" Emily

said urgently, through teeth that felt maybe a bit loose. Not the time to worry about that, right now, though.

Tyler bent down and removed the ropes from Emily's legs, taking a chance to evaluate her ankle while he was down there. It was swollen - much worse than before - and he wasn't sure she could put much weight on it. He noticed the pungent smell of urine from when she must have lost control of her bodily functions. It reminded him of his own urge to relieve himself. He thought it best not to mention this and moved to her hands, but as he went to pull on the ropes, they fell free.

"That's weird," he commented.

"What?"

"The ropes on your hands were barely tied. You probably could have been free hours ago."

Emily thought back to her communication with Carol. Maybe she really had tried to help her and just ran out of energy. Now being completely freed from the ropes, they decided to see how much weight her ankle could really hold. The release from the ropes and an upright body allowed her blood to flow freely once more.

But along with that came more pain, and she hit the floor quickly.

"Shit!" she let out as she collapsed back in the chair.

"It's ok! We'll figure something out. Maybe we can wrap it with something to keep pressure off. We just need it to function long enough for you to make it to the car." Tyler was unsure what to do. He hadn't thought about any extra obstacles and now he was running into multiple ones. His first thought was to use one of the jackets over on the workbench, but then it hit him. He had seen an Ace bandage on one of the bathroom shelves.

"Wait right here," he said, stiffly taking off up the ladder and then, with an extra effort, into the house.

"I'll be right here," she sighed, thinking: "Not like I can go anywhere."

Tyler navigated his way through the closet, up the stairs and into the bathroom. He knew he had adrenaline to thank for this sudden surge of energy, but his limbs still felt stiff and uncoordinated. Before grabbing the Ace bandage, he took the opportunity to relieve the painful pressure in his bladder he'd been suffering for an ungodly amount of time. He was quite surprised he hadn't wet himself by now, considering the circumstances. He thought of Emily and felt bad for her embarrassing situation. Finishing up as quickly as he could, he grabbed the bandage from the top shelf and staggered - but fast - back down to the basement, leaving the trapdoor open for an easy escape. Once he was by her side again, and was wrapping Emily's ankle as tightly as he could, she said:

"Why don't we just get out of here now? What is there in this plan that says we have to wait?"

"Because we can't let this go on. We have to stop them!"

"That's not our responsibility. Wasn't it you that wanted to go to the police? Let's do that. Come on! We'll go right now!"

"No! This is personal now. If you want to go, then go. But just remember the issues here. Where are you going? How are you going to get there?" Tyler pulled his hands from his jeans pockets. Hanging off his index finger was the key fob to his car.

"You had them this whole time!"

"I never go anywhere without my keys. Even if it's just the fob. No one can start the car without it. Thankfully, they didn't find it on me."

Tyler bent down under the workbench and grabbed Emily's phone. Before handing it to her, he checked the battery. There was barely enough charge to make one phone call as he had planned. He checked around for his phone and found it buried under a jacket. It was dead.

Tyler paced the floor as Emily remained seated. It was best that she stayed off her ankle until it was time to activate the plan. They went over detail after detail of what was about to take place. Emily tried to persuade him one last time to let it go and make a run for it, but he was hellbent on putting a stop to them once and for all.

"You're just going to go to jail for them?" she asked.

"Self-defense. They constrained us against our will. The evidence is all over this room - ropes, chairs, candles, blood… the other bodies. It's all down here."

Emily agreed he had a point. What she couldn't understand was why risk it. What if it didn't go as he'd planned. What if they never made it out of the basement?

Their conversation was quickly interrupted by the sound of footsteps coming down the tunnel. They shoved their phones into their back pockets and Emily straightened back up in the chair. Tyler hid behind the plywood door - his fingers wrapped tightly around one of the objects Lorelai had unknowingly gifted him.

Tyler heard the latch release and watched the door slowly open. He wasn't sure who was on the other side, but by the sounds of the footsteps, he expected it to be Lorelai. He was right. As she stepped into the room she panicked, realizing that Tyler was no longer in his chair - and Emily was free.

"The boy! Where is the boy?" she yelled as she rushed towards Emily. "Where is he? Tell me! Where is he?" Lorelai attempted to violently shake Emily.

"I don't know! I don't know!" she cried - the shaking had caused her to hit her ankle against the chair and sent violent stabs of pain shooting through her leg.

As Emily struggled to fight off Lorelai, Tyler stepped out from behind the door - a wrought iron candle holder gripped tightly in his hands. Before she knew it, Tyler took the hardest swing he could muster up and hit her over the head. She instantly fell to the floor.

"Go! Now!" he yelled at Emily and watched her jump out of the chair and hobble as best she could towards the trapdoor - grabbing the poker in passing.

Tyler knelt over to check Lorelai's pulse. It was there. Barely, but it was there. He was about to take one more swing when he heard Jeb coming through the tunnel.

"Shit!" he said to himself as he turned and ran out the back door towards the well. When he reached the end he looked back - but Jeb was nowhere to be seen. Tyler fought his way up the rickety ladder - his damaged knee now in agony again. Just before reaching the top a rung broke and he fell to the ground - hitting the lump on the back of his head as he landed. His body convulsed in agony - he lay there a moment in a daze. "Get up!" he told himself. "Get up now!" He let out a yell as he pulled himself back up. Everything was hurting. Thankfully, the ladder wasn't completely broken, and he made another attempt at getting out - this time testing each rung before trusting it with his weight.

When he reached the top, he rolled over and collapsed on the ground. His body was failing him fast. Where was Emily? Did she make it? He had to get up. He had to keep going. He took a deep breath and with everything he had left in him, pulled himself upright. Then as the dizziness ebbed away, he sprinted off for the car. As he came up on the driveway, he saw Emily attempting to run as best she could from the porch. Something was wrong. She wasn't heading towards the car. She was heading towards the road.

Emily had just exited the closet as Jeb began climbing up the ladder to the trap door. She slammed the door behind her, trying to slow him down, but as she turned to run through the living room her wounded foot tripped over a chair leg, and she fell to the floor. Pain - once again - reverberated through her leg, this time taking her a moment to regain the strength to get up. It wasn't long before Jeb - packed with his shotgun - barged through the closet door and was nearly on top of her.

Fighting to get away, she let out a guttural scream as she took the poker and jabbed it hard, right into the soft part of his thigh. He fell against the wall in pain, but this only made him angrier, letting out a demonic growl as he pulled the poker out of the raw meat of his thigh. It did, however, give her enough time to get back on her feet. She remembered her cell phone in her back pocket and immediately pulled it out to dial 911. But when she made it to the front door, it was locked. "The one damn time it wouldn't open on its own," she thought to herself while she frantically fought to get it open. Finally, it gave.

"God damnit!" she yelled as she emerged onto the porch, turning to see Jeb on her heels - slower now, but nevertheless trailing her closely. Then he stopped at the door, imposing his evil glare upon her. Emily hit the call button on her phone and took off running as best she could, her ankle wobbling agonizingly as she pushed on. Out of the corner of her eye she spotted Tyler coming around the house. She wasn't sure if he knew about the gun, but she did know that if she ran towards the car Jeb would take them both out. She decided to abort the plan. One of them getting away would be better than both dying. And after all, this was mostly her fault for not listening to Tyler in the first place. As she ran towards the tree line, cell clenched in her sweaty palm, she could hear the operator on the line.

"9-1-1. How can we help you? Hello? Is anyone there?"

"HHHHEEEEELLLLPPPP!!!!" Emily let out, just before the gunshot from the porch went off. It all happened so fast. She stopped in her tracks and dropped the phone on the ground. She looked down, seeing uncomprehendingly that blood was gushing from her abdomen. Realizing it was she who'd been shot - and not Tyler - gave her a slight sense of relief. But it was hard to focus now, with her lifeblood cascading out of a great ugly cavity in her guts. And where was Tyler? Her eyes were starting to blur. She pushed herself on closer to the tree line before collapsing.

Tyler ducked down behind the porch as he heard the gunshot. He watched Emily stop running and drop her phone - her body making its way to the ground played in slow motion like some kind of movie. His mind couldn't wrap around what was happening. Why didn't he take a dose of his own medicine and listen to *her* when she said they should escape when they had the chance? Now she'd been shot, and he didn't know whether she was still alive. Tears welled up in his eyes but he choked them down, trying to remain as quiet as possible. He wasn't sure where the gunshot had come from.

He decided to continue. He would immediately go to the closest safe place and call for help. He darted the few remaining feet to his car. Jumping in, he quickly started it and threw the gear shift in reverse. As he sped down the driveway, he noticed Jeb on the porch with the shotgun aimed right at him. He let out every curse word in his vocabulary and ducked down, expecting to dodge bullets - but then he saw him lower the gun. As the car reached the end of the driveway, Tyler heard the horns from a freight liner trying to warn him to stop. He slammed on the brakes, but it was too late. The car continued to roll into the curve. He quickly attempted to throw it back in drive, but before his hand could reach the gearshift, the sound of squealing brakes and metal crunching against metal engulfed him - until all was silent.

Tyler found himself outside the car looking down at the poor thing, now irrevocably smashed to pieces. He was amazed he had made it out unscathed - and actually feeling strangely ok - but as he walked round to the front, his mind refused to recognize what he saw…

As expected, there was a lot of mangled metal. He briefly wondered if his beloved car was even salvageable. It would cost him a fortune to have it fixed - even if it were possible. But it would also cost a lot to have this mess towed away. An abundance of finances was not something he had, and he was unsure what procedures needed to be taken. Would his insurance even begin to cover it?

But as his eyes traveled over the wreck just inches before him, all worries about insurance rapidly dissipated. He must have had a passenger. Well, clearly, he did, because there he was… the poor sap… smashed up against the windshield, an ear hanging off, nose obliterated, tufts of hair missing, one eye half out… blood everywhere. This guy would never worry about insurance, that's for sure, ever again.

It must be the shock. It must be the shock that wiped his memory of having a passenger. But as he forced himself to stare at the hideous mess that had been a man, Tyler realized he looked familiar. Only too familiar.

There was no mysterious passenger, was there? Look, the guy's in the driver's seat.

"Tyler, Tyler, Tyler… it's happened. It's actually happened," he thought to himself. "That's you there. Or what's left of you. You're a dead man. A dead man walking. Welcome to the afterlife." This was a huge thought. Not one he expected to have for many years to come. But here he was.

He tried to move - it was easy. Just his feet were touching the road, but he couldn't feel it. But when he tried to touch the car, his hand - his curiously glowing, slightly transparent hand - went through it. No traction. So that was true, too. He was one hell of a cliched ghost…*Ghost*…But as he thought the word, the whole horror of his situation overwhelmed him.

"HELP!!! HELP ME!!" he screamed. "HELP ME!!!" But his voice sounded thin and flat, and somehow, he knew that no one had heard him. Maybe no one could hear him ever again.

Tyler heard sirens coming towards him. He stepped out into the street to flag them down, as if they couldn't see the massive wreck in the middle of the road. Then his thoughts turned to Emily… Emily! No one's going to know to look for Emily with all of this mess here. He screamed again:

"HELP ME!!! PLEASE!!! PLEASE HELP MY FRIEND!!! SHE'S OVER THERE!!!"

"Hey, man! No one can hear you," a strange voice said.

Tyler quickly turned around to see a tall, blond, and handsome young man about twenty-five standing behind him. Tyler blinked. At least that still worked. Then it dawned on him…

"Wait! I know you! You're Andrew. You're dead!" Tyler exclaimed, as one of the fire trucks drove through his iridescent body. He shook off the strange but momentary discomfort - it was rather like being impaled on a stuffed toy - and asked: "What just happened?"

"Why don't you move over here?" Andrew suggested, motioning Tyler to get out of the road. "I'll try to explain as much as I can."

"I don't have time for explanations right now. I have to save my friend. She's been shot. She's right over there. Please, come help me."

"Man, you've really got to calm down. There's nothing you can do. *You're* dead."

Tyler stopped - his spirit letting out a deep sigh. The heaviness of everything that had just happened sunk in. Come on, man, admit it properly. He was a ghost. He had become the thing he had once hunted. He started to feel dizzy… then questioned: "Can spirits feel dizzy?"

"It can happen when too much energy is used. I'd

say you've used up a whole other lifetime of energy in the last five minutes," Andrew solemnly replied. There wasn't much inflection in his voice. It reminded Tyler of the sound of an EVP - breathy or winded.

As more emergency vehicles began to arrive, Tyler noticed a face amongst the crowd that he'd wished he hadn't. The face - along with his broad-shouldered body - took off into the darkness. "Where did he come from?" Tyler thought to himself and started to follow him. Andrew walked slowly behind him - observing his every move. Tyler saw the man come to a stop in the area where Emily had dropped to the ground and began searching around for something. The face bent down and picked up Emily's phone and slid it into his overalls. Then Tyler watched as he moved over to Emily's body. He loomed over her briefly before kneeling beside her.

Tyler's world was spinning around him. There was so much going on. So much he was picking up on. Being a ghost was like sensory overload. Not having a physical body was like having all your filters removed without warning. Everything was raw and immediate. He heard the driver of the freight liner that had plowed into his car giving a report to a local sheriff. Apparently, he had made it out alive. Lucky bastard. He heard emergency workers leaving the house talking over their radios about how they were carrying out two male bodies in multiple pieces. He also heard them say that the house was all clear. Where was Lorelai? Why hadn't they brought her out? She must have survived. Not the outcome he had wanted, but - hey! - now at least he could haunt her for the rest of her life. It wasn't much of a comforting thought, but right now it was all he had.

When he refocused his mind on the familiar face, he discovered him still kneeling over Emily's body. Tyler turned to Andrew, who placed his hand on Tyler's shoulder in an attempt to get him to turn away.

"Don't watch this. I made the mistake of watching this when they did it to Carol. It's not something you want to remember."

"I… can't… just leave her there. It's my fault she's…" Tyler said, noticing his own inflection voice was fading.

"You have to," Andrew interrupted, taking Tyler by the shoulders, and turning him around.

Tyler could hear Emily at first struggling to get away, then struggling to breathe. He tried to reach her through his mind. Trying to let her know it would be ok. *Would it?* He thought. When it was over, Andrew turned him back around. Tyler was all impatient and anxious, sort-of standing there on the front lawn looking in the opposite direction - not being able to help his terribly hurt friend. But turning around slowly, dread rising, Tyler witnessed Emily's spirit rise out of her body.

Tyler and Andrew stood as Emily looked around the area, looking lost at first before focusing on the image of her lifeless body sprawled out on the ground - lying in a pool of blood and with a face that had turned blue from suffocation. They could tell she was starting to get emotional.

"Hey! Ova here! Got 'nother one!" The three of them heard Jeb call out. As the responders ran over, he tucked himself into the woods and disappeared.

Emily sat with herself as the medical team did all

they could to revive her, but she knew it was too late. Nothing could be done. Memories of the last twenty-four hours came rushing back in and she started looking around - searching for something to latch on to. She could see an accident had occurred on the bend, but with it being dark, it was too hard to tell what had actually happened. It was then that she saw someone familiar.

"Tyler!" She jumped up and rushed towards him with arms wide open. It took her a moment to realize that if she could see him and he could see her, something was wrong. She paused in front of him - tilting her head - and he pointed toward the wreck at the end of the driveway. If she'd had a heart, it would have sunk to the ground. But apparently, remorse was something the dead could still feel.

"I'm so sorry!" she said, tears starting to fall down her ghostly face. "It was a good plan. We did our best."

"No! I should have listened to you. We should have run when we first had the chance. I'm the one who should be sorry," Tyler empathized.

Andrew stood by, watching them embrace in a

ghostly hug - the iridescent glow surrounding them as one unified light. As Emily's memory continued to flood her mind, she turned to Andrew, whom she recognized from her research of the past week and said:

"So, what now? I guess we are stuck here?" she asked.

"Yeah, unfortunately, it seems so," Andrew replied. "Come with me. Come meet everyone. Might as well since you've been trying to connect with us for the past week."

Gliding along just above the path, Emily and Tyler entered the house once again, this time seeing it from a different perspective. As they passed the emergency responders Andrew explained that while human entities could be seen or heard, ghostly entities could not unless they wanted to be. This gave them a sense of safety in the house for once. As they entered the kitchen everyone was sitting around the island - Carol, Jeremy, and Mary. Mr. Nichols sat across in the dining room working on a crossword puzzle in a 1929 newspaper.

"Welcome to the house!" Mrs. Nichols said, stretching out her arms to give each of them hugs.

"Thank you!" Emily replied hesitantly - yet the hug from Mrs. Nichols felt warm and welcoming. The longer she held her, the more her hesitancy faded away. "We have so many questions."

"Ask away, dear. Now that we can finally answer them. Plus, we have all the time in the world."

Tyler spoke up before Emily had a chance to even think. Apparently, personalities do not change when you are a ghost. "Why didn't you all help us when we asked, begged, and pleaded for your help?"

"Oh, honey, we gave you everything you needed to get out of this house before tonight," Carol spoke up, "Why, even the recording on that little machine was a complete reenactment of tonight. Well, as complete as we could make it. Sometimes we don't get all the information. See where you went wrong is that you thought it was a reenactment of Andrew and I - when in fact, it was the two of you. Oh! And I did loosen those ropes a bit."

"And what about Lilith? Where is she?" Emily inquired, knowing she had seen two different forms of her the night before. “And why does she look like me?”

Mrs. Nichols raised her hand and said, “I’ll take this one!” She positioned herself at the end of the island like she was standing at the head of a table. She was just as Emily had imagined her - like a 1920s’ socialite… only a more country version. “You see, dear. I sent you those visions, or whatever you want to call them, last night. It’s no wonder you didn’t pick up on the message, considering all the stress the two of you were under.” She took a sip out of her wine glass and continued: “You remember that Lorelai told you a male sacrifice was needed? Well, can you remember one occasion when that didn’t happen? No?”

She didn’t give them time to answer and continued: “It was me. When I used Lilith's hand to take my life, it broke the agreement made between the Sullivans and whatever devil they made a deal with, which is why they have continued to suffer ever since. I knew the house wouldn’t remain in their possession if the agreement was broken. These people have just been murdering people for the hell of it since then. It’s in their blood. It’s in their nature. As for Lilith, she is not welcomed here, though she makes an appearance from time to time - and only around Halloween. The only reason she would be showing herself to you would be that she is a terrible monster who is able to transform into whatever she wants to destroy people's lives."

"That sounds like the whole family of Sullivans," Tyler took a moment to chime in.

"I'll tell you what," Mrs. Nichols said, looking at Emily and Tyler, "For all your ghosthunter friends out there: Sometimes it's better if they'd pay more attention to what is actually haunting them. You never know. We might be trying to help them. Or they could be completely clueless and end up like you two."

Everyone around the island burst into loud laughter as one of the emergency workers was doing a final check of the house. Approaching the front door, he turned back to look towards the kitchen. He could have sworn he heard laughter, but the house had already been cleared and no one was supposed to be inside. Turning into the kitchen, he saw that no one was present. He chalked it up to his imagination until he walked out on the porch and one of the rocking chairs was moving on its own. He asked around if anyone had sat in any of the chairs on the porch, but everyone replied "no".

Epilogue

One Year Later…

Dawn and Kit pulled onto the grounds of the old two-story farmhouse. It was rundown and hadn't been taken very good care of over the past year. They were running behind as usual, but the rest of the team were already there when they arrived. Exiting the car, they grabbed the memorial wreath they had planned to place on the side of the road in memory of their fellow team member and leader.

Another new member, John, approached them as they walked towards the rickety porch. Dawn had recruited John after taking over as team leader last year. She and Emily had been friends for a long time, and she felt it was necessary to continue with Emily's dream of documenting the paranormal.

"I don't like the energy of this place," John said, walking up onto the porch. "Do we even have permission to be here? It looks abandoned."

"We're fine. I cleared it with the city before we came down," Kit responded.

"I don't know… something's not right here."

Kit - more properly known as Jared on a more professional level - was now married to Dawn and had taken on the task of running the team's tech. It wasn't something he was passionate about, just what he did. The nickname came from his obsession with cars - sports cars especially. Everyone started calling him Kit when he purchased an old Pontiac Firebird Trans Am that looked just like a replica from the show *Knight Rider* back in the mid 80's.

John, on the other hand, was brought in as the team's resident psychic. He tended to be really good at reading energies. At times he was able to communicate with spirits on the other side - visually and telepathically.

And it wasn't very often that he was wrong. It was fairly common for him to see random spirits throughout the day wherever he was. Dawn had decided to bring him along on this trip in hopes of being able to connect with Emily and Tyler.

Cassey and Amber had recently joined the team. They were coworkers of Dawn's and decided to tag along for emotional support. They were always willing to assist whenever there was a need. Cassey had even met Emily a few times in passing.

"Ok, team!" Dawn called brightly, corralling everyone up close to the porch. "Everyone let's keep our watch up. This house is rundown, and I really don't want to take any of you to the hospital tonight. Please be safe! We're going to do our memorial here in just a moment. I want to do that before it gets dark, since we'll be close to the highway. Once it's dark, no one is allowed to go near the road. Do you understand? This is for your own safety."

"Yes," everyone replied.

"Ok! We're going to let John do a walkthrough of

the house, just before we get started. John, would you like to come with me? I'll record your reactions as we go through the house."

Dawn and John entered the building while the others waited outside. It was the first time for both of them since the horrible incident last year. John's immediate impression was that there was a woman present who was trying to communicate with him.

"Ok, what is she saying?" Dawn asked.

"I'm not sure. I keep hearing 'a tidy house keeps the devils at bay.' She's just saying it over and over."

"I don't see anything tidy about this house. The furniture has holes in it from rodents, the floors are filthy, and there's no electricity anymore."

"Let's move on. I'm not really getting a good vibe from her."

"Ok. Why don't we head upstairs?"

They walked up the stairs, rounding the corner facing the front of the house. They entered the bedroom on the right. It was obvious that it used to be some sort of library, though most of the books had been removed or were scattered all over the floor.

"I'm getting the image of an older man sitting in one of these chairs. He's got salt and pepper hair with a receding hairline. He appears to be holding a book in one hand and a cigar in the other."

"That's interesting. That sounds like Mr. Nichols, though I'm not sure if he smoked or not. Is he saying anything to you?"

"Not at the moment. He appears to be ignoring us. Let's move on. We can try to reach out to him later on when he's hopefully not so preoccupied."

Moving across the hall, they entered the master bedroom.

"Oh, the woman in here is feisty! She's a bit of a tomboy and doesn't take anyone's shit. That's what I'm getting. She doesn't take anyone's shit."

"Yep, that sounds like our Emily. Hey, girl! It's me, Dawn! I'm here!"

"She says she knows who you are and that she has a warning for you."

"A warning? What kind of warning?"

"She says it's not safe here. There's evil around tonight and that everyone should pack up and leave."

"Oh, Emily! You're always trying to tell us what to do - even in death." Dawn chuckled indulgently at the thought. "I'm sure we'll be fine, girl."

"I don't think we should take her so ligh…" John tried to relay his concerns but was quickly interrupted by Dawn.

"Is there anywhere else you're feeling drawn to in the house?"

"The basement. I think I wanna go down to the basement." John watched the ghostly image of Emily shaking her head "no" as they turned to walk out of the room.

"I'm not sure we can get down there, but we can try."

They headed back down the stairs and towards the living room closet. Dawn had heard about the trapdoor on the news but wasn't sure it would still be accessible. As she opened the door, she was able to see that the trapdoor was still intact. Probably one of the only things still intact in this house. She found it odd that a modern-day ladder was now in place of the wooden one she knew about, but they continued down anyway.

"Oh! This is bad. There's something really bad down here."

"What is it? Can you tell?"

"I don't think this is a human spirit. It's something much darker than that. Much much darker. I'm getting… 'you made a deal with me, and I want my payment.' That's what I keep hearing."

"Oh, wow! I wonder who made a deal? We may have to come back down here and see if we can find out. It's starting to get late. Maybe we should head back upstairs to the group and get ready for the ceremony. I think we've had enough of this creepy basement for now."

As they made their way back through the trapdoor, they heard the sound of glasses clanging and party chatter through the wall. They followed it to what appeared to be a disappointingly empty kitchen. Dawn searched around the rest of the house and checked outside to see if anyone else could have been responsible for the noises. When she reentered the hallway outside the kitchen, the cupboard door popped open. She immediately knew who this was as it was a cupboard under the stairs.

"Hi, Tyler!" she said, "Hope you are doing well. We'll be back in later in the night. Please feel free to come and chat with us." She pushed the door closed before finding her way back to John in the kitchen.

"The lady of the house is having a party tonight."

"Oh, was that what we heard?"

"I believe so. Come on. Let's go meet up with the others."

They backed out of the kitchen and walked out onto the porch, giving one more look around before gathering the team at the bend of the curve.

Kit carried the wreath, and everyone followed behind him. What everyone other than John didn't know was that the resident ghosts were also following. It seemed Mrs. Nichols had moved her party to the roadside, too. John was able to see the light-filled forms of Mrs. Nichols, Carol, Andrew, Jeremy, Emily, and Tyler as they walked out behind the rest.

"Everyone is here with us. They wanted me to let you all know that they are so honored you have chosen this beautiful wreath and flowers to pay your respects," John mentioned to the others.

"Oh, good!" Dawn said, as she helped Kit place the wreath just in the bend of the curve - far enough away so that traffic wouldn't damage it. Dawn read a touching speech that brought Emily's spirit to tears. Cassey and Amber each laid a bundle of roses they'd brought with them down at the base of the wreath stand. It was a beautiful ceremony and John felt that the spirits of the house were pleased. Well, at least the ones that attended. He stood still watching each one of the spirits fade away. The last to go were Emily and Tyler. They both gave a smile and a wave goodbye - slowly fading in with the country backdrop. John turned to mention that they had waved goodbye, but found he was the only one standing at the road.

The team had already headed back toward the house to get ready for their night's investigation. They unloaded their equipment - they'd packed light since there wasn't any power - flashlights and digital recorder were going to be their best friends for the evening. Unbeknownst to any member of the team, as they entered the house, they were being watched. Not by the ghosts, but by the tall, broad-shouldered man lurking in the distance - blending in with the tree line…

ABOUT THE AUTHOR

Jason Roach is a core member of the Association of Paranormal Study where he has written several blogs. His enthusiasm for the paranormal and personal experiences inspired him to incorporate them into this fictional tale. He has previously been a guest at ConCarolinas and GalaxyCon where he has provided insight on panels and has given presentations on the paranormal.

Originally born and raised in Statesville, NC, Jason moved to Winston-Salem in 2010 where he obtained two associates degrees in Business and Finance. He will complete his bachelor's in accounting in the fall of 2022. He is also a member of the IAPO Independent Book Publishing Professionals. He is in the process of opening his own publishing company catering for LGBTQIA+ authors.

When he's not tending to schoolwork, investigating the paranormal or working on the next big project, he enjoys spending time with his husband, Sean, and his two cats - Gandalf and Lyma - and doggy, Laylah. He enjoys traveling and visiting all things paranormal wherever his journeys take him.

Contact the Author

Facebook:

https://www.facebook.com/JasonRoachAuthor

Instagram:

@jasonroachauthor

Twitter:

@JRoachAuthor

TikTok:

@jasonroachauthor

Email:

JasonRoachAuthor@gmail.com